OPERATION JUGGERNAUT

A NOVEL

JUDITH BLEVINS

AND

CARROLL MULTZ

Judith Blevins

Carroll Multz

NEW!

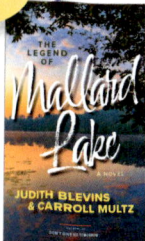

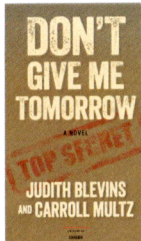

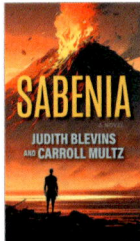

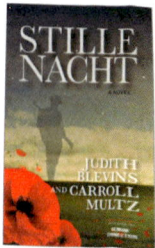

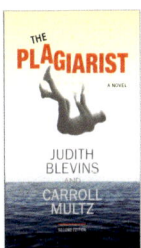

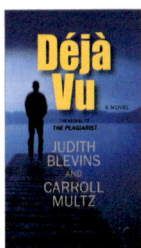

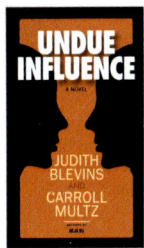

Operation Juggernaut

Published by
ShahrazaD Publishing®
2189 W Canyon Court
Grand Junction, CO 81507-2574

ISBN – 979-889589122-3

Contact the authors at:
judyblevins@bresnan.net
carrollmultz@charter.net

ALSO BY THE AUTHORS

Novels

By Judith Blevins

Double Jeopardy · Swan Song
Legacy · Karma · Paragon

By Carroll Multz

Justice Denied · Deadly Deception · License to Convict
The Devil's Scribe · The Chameleon
Shades of Innocence · The Winning Ticket

By Judith Blevins & Carroll Multz

Rogue Justice · The Plagiarist (First Edition)
A Desperate Plea · Spiderweb · The Méjico Connection
Eyewitness · Lust for Revenge · Kamanda · Bloodline
Pickpocket · Ghost Writer · Guilt by Innuendo
Gypsy Card Reader · Waves of Vengeance
Veil of Deceit · The Journalist · We the Jury · Star Chamber
Reflection of a Killer · Bonsai · The Gemini Connection
Stille Nacht · The Plagiarist (Second Edition)
Déjà Vu · Undue Influence · Sabenia
Don't Give Me Tomorrow · The Legend of Mallard Lake

Childhood Legends Series®

By Judith Blevins & Carroll Multz

Operation Cat Tale · One Frightful Day · Blue
The Ghost of Bradbury Mansion · White Out
Flash of Red · Back in Time · Treasure Seekers
Summer Vacation-Part 1: Castaways-Part 2: Blast Off
A Trip to Remember —The R*U*1*2s Journey
to the Nation's Capital

Dedication

*To those who risk their lives
to defend America.*

Do good to those who hate you,
bless those who curse you,
and pray for those who mistreat you.

Scripture

TABLE OF CONTENTS

A Note from the Authors 11

Chapter One: **Situation** 13

Chapter Two: **Indoctrination** 21

Chapter Three: **Infiltration** 37

Chapter Four: **Observation** 55

Chapter Five: **Preparation** 69

Chapter Six: **Insubordination** 81

Chapter Seven: **Detonation** 93

Chapter Eight: **Retaliation** 111

Chapter Nine: **Extraction** 123

Chapter Ten: **Implementation** 139

Chapter Eleven: **Navigation** 153

Chapter Twelve: **Trepidation** 167

Chapter Thirteen: **Transportation** 181

Chapter Fourteen: **Destination** 203

Chapter Fifteen: **Conclusion** 213

A Note From The Authors

In March of 1938, after being invaded by Germany, Austria voted to be annexed by their conquerors. It was a bitter pill to swallow by many but it was better than being decimated or completely wiped off the map. As the old adage says: "If you can't beat 'em, join 'em.

Germany considered it providential to expand its boundary on all four sides by force. One country after another was swallowed up by the German might. Austria was just the first. Fighting on all fronts with their neighboring countries, and ultimately non-contiguous nations which eventually included America, Germany was spread thin.

With journalistic liberty on the part of your authors, military equipment and personnel were provided to Germany by Austria, not *over* the Bavarian Alps, but *through* the mountain on the border of the two countries by way of a secret passage that was burrowed through the majestic mountain range.

Operation Juggernaut was the name of the mission designed to paralyze the German war effort. Two American soldiers, known simply as Wagner and Becker, with the help of a foreign agent, Lina, were assigned the task to take down the passageway.

We invite you to hop aboard the rollercoaster with the saboteurs. They'll take you on a ride you won't soon forget.

Special thanks to Jan Weeks for her editing skills, Frank Addington for the cover and interior book designs, and Rosalie Stewart and John Lukon of KC Book Manufacturing for printing *Operation Juggernaut*, and finally to our readers, as always, you continue to be our inspiration.

Chapter One

Situation

Five Star General Tobias "Toby" Rochester of the Army/Air Force and Defense Secretary Leonard "Leo" Perkins sat across from each other in an office near the War Room in the building known as the National Military Command. The venetian blinds in the second story office were partially opened and the lights from the Washington Monument could be seen in the distance. The hour was late and all government employees had left for the day. The only noise in the building was that generated by the janitorial staff as they made their rounds.

The two men were engaged in a covert meeting. General Rochester sat with his legs crossed, nervously tapping his ever-present swagger stick against his boot.

Secretary Perkins retrieved a half-empty bottle of scotch from his lower desk drawer and poured a generous amount of liquor into two water glasses. Handing one to the general, Perkins said in a raspy voice, "Toby, we have a dire situation we need to address."

Rochester had already surmised there was something amiss because of being asked to attend a covert after-hours meeting with the defense secretary. Reacting to the urgency in Perkins' voice, Rochester ceased tapping his boot and sat up straighter, giving the defense secretary his undivided attention. "What's that, Leo?" He asked with concern in his voice. From past experience, Rochester knew that Perkins was not one to shout "wolf" unless there was one.

Perkins furrowed his brow and studied the amber liquid in his glass for a moment before answering. Clearing his throat, he said, "Intelligence sources just learned that the Germans have hoodwinked the Allies."

"Not again! What happened and how bad is it?" Rochester asked, now on full alert with mounting concern evident in his voice.

"You remember a couple of months ago we discussed the dilemma of how the 'Jerrys' were always able to have an ample supply of weapons and ammunition on their front lines without prior notice of any such movements?"

"Hell, yes, I remember. They were kicking ass. For some inexplicable reason, they always seemed to be a jump ahead of the Allies," Rochester replied. "Exactly! Well, yesterday a plum fell into our laps. The Brits captured two Nazi soldiers close to the base of the Bavarian Alps that separate Austria from Germany in an area known as the Needles."

"Sure! I'm familiar with the Needles…"

"Well, hold onto your hat! As you know, Austria aligned with Germany early in the war. The two captured prisoners revealed that since the Austrians sided with the Nazis, the Austrians helped Germany widen the corridor through the Needles, making it large enough to move supplies from the Austrian side to the German side without having to cross the summit. We learned that the Austrians were manufacturing war materials on their side of the Alps and supplying them to the Germans by way of the Needles."

"What! How—"

Raising a hand, Perkins continued, "That was the Brit commander's question so he sent a team of moles in to verify the revelation. The prisoners' story held up."

"Well, I'll be damned!" Rochester muttered, leaning forward and holding up his glass for a refill. "Here we thought the Alps were benign and of no consequence as far as the war was concerned."

Pouring another round for both, Perkins continued, "To answer your unasked question, the moles also determined that the corridor appeared to be as well protected as Fort Knox, indicating something major was afoot. Because of the location, it would be nearly impossible to penetrate from land or air."

Swirling the liquor around in his glass, Rochester didn't look up when he asked, "What are our options?" He was a seasoned old bird and knew where there was a will, there was a way.

"You mean other than a miracle?" Perkins muttered.

"Unless you have that miracle up your sleeve, what's your backup plan?" Rochester asked. All types of scenarios were already whirling around in his head.

Perkins retorted, "That's why you're here. I don't share my scotch with just anybody."

"I'm flattered," Rochester said. "Go on."

"If we can seal off that pipeline, it would severely handicap the Germans. I respect your judgment and experience and wanted to bounce my thoughts off you."

"Okay, I'm all ears." Rochester replied.

Rearing back in his worn leather desk chair and plopping his feet up on his desk, Perkins looked up at the ceiling for a moment, apparently collecting his thoughts before beginning to relate his Trojan Horse theory. "I was thinking that if we could get a few spies into the German ranks, they could plant enough explosives to cave in the corridor, thus blocking the route, at least for a while anyway. If we get lucky, the whole mountain might fall, completely obliterating the passage and any war machinery and supplies stored inside."

Rochester grunted. "Sounds like you've been watching too many John Wayne movies. The miracle you mentioned might be easier to come by than I first thought—"

"Hold on, pilgrim, I'm not finished yet," Perkins interrupted. "I just gave you a rough sketch. The team we select must speak fluent German and have at least one explosive expert. We have some pretty resourceful people in our military, we just need to get them inside. We have civilian interpreters who speak fluent German—" said Perkins.

Now it was Rochester's turn to interrupt. "True, but they haven't been through boot camp. It would take at least three months to get them in shape, much less embark on a mission like the one you're suggesting. From what you tell me, time is not on our side."

"I thought of that, too. However, the opposition is intuitive and I prefer to opt on the side of caution. How could we ferret out trained soldiers who speak fluent German without arousing suspicion?" Perkins asked. "I hate to say it, but you know the enemy has spies everywhere—even in our own military."

Rochester nodded. "How well I know." After a pause, he added, "Okay, I'm listening. Everything is on the table. What are you proposing?"

Perkins was silent for a few moments, obviously in deep reflection over what he was about to say. Even though Rochester said everything was on the table, he hoped Rochester wouldn't consider his proposal outlandish.

Perkins finally cleared his throat and said, "In order to expedite the mission, we could manufacture a new division and open it to enlistment from our existing ranks. We could call it, for example, Select Operations Forces. Adding the phrase, 'What foreign languages do you speak?' to the application form shouldn't raise suspicion. When we interview those who apply, we can dig deeper into their language skills. Since those now enlisted have already gone through boot camp, we save at least three months. What do you think?"

Perkins was surprised, as well as relieved, when Rochester sat up and whacked his boot with his swagger stick, replying, "I like it, Leo. I like it a lot. And I like the name you suggested, Select Operations Forces."

"That does have a nice ring to it. Since you acquiesce, I'll put the wheels in motion first thing tomorrow morning. We don't have a minute to waste."

The two men stood and shook hands. Rochester slapped Perkins on the shoulder and said, "You'll have my full cooperation and that of my staff."

Chapter Two

Indoctrination

Jackson "Jack" Becker was sitting on his bunk cleaning his fingernails with his pocketknife. Several other off-duty soldiers were lounging about. Some were playing cards or writing letters, others were sprawled on their bunks just relaxing. Everyone snapped to attention when the division's sergeant burst into the barracks. The sergeant executed a weak salute and mumbled, "At ease." He was carrying a file folder and a hammer. The soldiers watched as he nailed an announcement to the door. When he finished, he looked around the barracks and grunted, "As you were," and left. Becker went to the door and read the announcement.

"What's it say?" PFC Clay McCallister asked, as he sat up on his bunk.

"Looks like a recruitment notification of some kind," Becker replied. "Select Operations Forces. Whatever that is."

"Never heard of 'em," McCallister said and plopped back down.

Overhearing the conversation, PFC Lowell Wagner sat up, swinging his legs over the edge of his cot. "What's it all about?" he asked.

"Don't know, but if it means better rations and living quarters, count me in," Becker said.

"Hell, yes!" said Wagner. "Let's go find out."

• • •

When Wagner and Becker arrived at the sergeant's office, they were surprised at the number of men standing in line. "Looks like we're not the only ones interested in the new division," Wagner said. Just as he finished his remark, PFC Frank Tolson came out of the sergeant's office. He took the steps two at a time and appeared to be in a hurry.

"Hold on, Tolson," Becker called after him. "What's going on?"

"Oh, the brass is lookin' for new interpreters. They're pretty picky. Want you to know all the colloquialisms and stuff like that in German. Me? I can cuss in German with the best of 'em. That's my specialty because of being reamed out so often by my dad when I goofed up," Tolson responded. "Otherwise, forget it. Even my English ain't that great, much less German."

Becker looked at Wagner, "What'd you think?" he asked.

"My dad worked in the Virginia coal mines alongside many German Americans," Wagner replied. "I learned to speak German before I spoke

English. When I was old enough, I took my turn in the mines. Didn't take long for me to decide that wasn't my bag. Don't like being underground, especially when using explosives. Interpreting sounds interesting. How bad can it be? I'm game, how 'bout you?" Little did he know at the time what he was getting into.

"Yeah, me, too. My pop took off when I was born, leaving my mom to raise my two older sisters and me. Mom eventually married a German immigrant. He adopted us three kids and treated us decently. He worked in a grocery store in the Bronx, spoke Italian, English and German fluently. He even taught us to speak German and Italian. He was very industrious. People like him and he eventually ended up owning the store. I wasn't interested in getting into the grocery business so I joined the Army." After a pause, he added, "Mom died two years ago."

After about ten minutes of waiting in line, when it was Wagner's turn to interview, a burly drill sergeant stuck his head out of the office door and shouted, "Next!"

• • •

Back at the barracks, after their interviews, Wagner and Becker compared notes. "How'd it go?" Becker asked.

"Not sure. Everyone who interviewed me seemed noncommittal," Wagner said. "They got really excited when I told them *Ich sprechen sie Deutsch* and that I was familiar with the use of dynamite from having worked in the coal mines. I thought they were going to wet their britches."

"Very strange! Wonder what that's all about?" Becker mused.

"Don't know, but you know the old saying, 'yours is not to reason why'…"

"Yup, I'm familiar with that one. It's the 'do or die' part I'm concerned about," Becker mused.

"Well, at least you'll still have three hots and a cot," Wagner joked.

"So do convicted serial killers…"

Before lights out, Wagner and Becker were informed by their sergeant that they had been selected to be the interpreters.

"Transport is picking you guys up tomorrow… early, so be ready."

Stunned at all the informality, Wagner and Becker just looked at each other. Finally, Wagner said, "Come on, let's get our shit together." After a pause, he added, "Wonder how many more they recruited?"

"Guess we'll find out soon enough."

• • •

Wagner and Becker were ready at 6:00 a.m. Their transport took them to an airfield where a plane was already revving up. They were hustled aboard as soon as their Jeep stopped. When they entered the cabin, much to their surprise, they noticed they were the only recruits on the plane. Once they were seated, and the plane began to taxi for takeoff, an officer stood and addressed them.

"Good morning, gentlemen. I'm Corporal Manning and I will be your tour guide throughout your Select Forces basic training. Because of the nature of your mission, you will be stationed at an undisclosed base for security purposes. Until the mission is concluded, you'll not receive or send mail. In case you're wondering, only the two of you will embark on this mission. The fewer people who know, the better off you'll be. The mission consists of the use of unconventional warfare—"

Wagner's hand shot up.

"Yes, what is it?" Manning asked, irritation evident in his voice.

"Pardon me for interrupting, sir," Wagner said, "but we thought we were going to be interpreters. No one said anything about warfare, much less *unconventional warfare.*"

"That's correct," Manning said. "However, we have a critical situation on the German-Austrian border. That's all I'm authorized to tell you at this time. If you'll be patient, all the pieces will fall into place."

Wagner looked at Becker. Becker just shrugged and sank lower into his seat.

"As I was saying," Manning continued, "The two of you were cleared before being selected for this mission. It was determined that your credentials meet the requirements, and as you may have guessed by now, the mission is critical, extremely dangerous, and highly confidential. You're scheduled for a briefing as soon as we land.

"I've been authorized to inform you that, after hearing the details of the mission, if you refuse to participate, you will be placed in solitary confinement in a military prison until the war is over." After a pause, Manning added, "Does that give you an idea of how critical and confidential this operation is?"

Because of Manning's attitude and the "critical and highly confidential" nature of the mission, Wagner and Becker didn't speak during the remainder of the trip.

Solitary confinement in a military prison until the war ended? thought Wagner. It appeared that a line had been drawn in the sand and they didn't dare cross it. Discretion was the better part of valor.

• • •

When they landed at the undisclosed airfield, Wagner and Becker were taken to a barracks and instructed to store their gear and freshen up, all the while under the watchful eye of Corpoal. Manning. There was no sign of anyone else having occupied the barracks. It was obvious they were the only two occupants. Still stunned, and not knowing what to expect, the two maintained their silence. The cloak and dagger attitude was becoming unnerving.

A Jeep and driver were waiting outside the barracks. Accompanied by Manning, they were driven to the main building and ushered into an office. Manning retreated, closing the door behind him. A five star general stood and greeted them.

The general said, "I'm General Rochester. I recognize the two of you from the pictures in your files. I'm here to explain to you the nature of our top-secret mission, please come in and take a seat."

"Thank you, sir," they said in unison, now even more confused than ever by being briefed by a general.

After they were seated, the general turned and pulled down a map that was suspended from the ceiling. Using his swagger stick as a pointer, he began the briefing.

"This is a map of the mountain range on the

German-Austrian border known as the Bavarian Alps. Since Austria supports German policies, they willingly allow Germany to use the border crossing between the two countries to store and transport supplies that are being manufactured in Austria.

"Right here," the general pointed to the base of the mountain and tapped the map with his swagger stick, "is an area known as the Needles. The Needles has a small natural tunnel spanning approximately half a mile between the two countries. It was just wide enough for a man to walk through from one side to the other. We recently learned that the Germans widened the tunnel, making it accessible for storing supplies, ammunition, and equipment and moving them from the Austrian side of the mountain to the German side."

Moving to a table, the general motioned for Wagner and Becker to follow. "Come closer," he urged. "We were unable to obtain pictures of the interior of the tunnel. However, we do have a rough diagram of the layout." The general paused. "In case you're wondering how we accomplished that, we infiltrated an ally, code name Shadow, into the facility. Shadow is well entrenched and has earned the trust of the Germans."

The general sat down. Wagner and Becker followed. The general continued with his briefing.

"It's not complicated. Our mission is very simple, blow up the tunnel and everything, including the explosives, stored there. The two of you are unique because you speak conversational German and chances of your arousing suspicion are slim. Also, PFC Wagner, with you having previously worked in coal mines, which is much like the target tunnel, you're qualified as an explosives expert. The combination of language and knowledge of explosives are a rare commodity."

Wagner looked at Becker. *Is this some kind of joke?*

Feeling like the sacrificial lamb, Becker interrupted, "Pardon me, sir," he said. "We were under the impression we were going to be used as interpreters—"

Showing impatience, the general said, "Surely, you understand why we couldn't advertise the nature of the mission. Your duty now is to follow orders…or spend the rest of the war in solitary confinement in a military prison!"

Becker shrank back. Suddenly, the gravity of the situation hit him. He looked at Wagner. Wagner's expression told Becker that he too, was shocked.

"Well?" The general barked, as he waited for an answer.

Becker gulped. He knew all too well how those

suspected of being cowards were treated in prison. "I'm in," he muttered.

The general glared at Wagner.

"Me, too," Wagner said.

"Good! You will be infiltrated as German officers. We'll spend the next two weeks training you on how to act like a German officer. Shadow has arranged for the two of you to share quarters and will acquaint you with the area." Looking sternly at Wagner and Becker, the general added, "From this moment until the mission is completed, you will speak only German. You must, for your own safety get into the habit of using only the German language. One small slip and you're dead, and most likely, you'll be tortured before they kill you. The Nazis show no mercy and leave no margin for error."

Becker looked at Wagner. The blood was draining from Wagner's face and he was turning very pale. The general ignored the reaction and continued. "You will be here at this facility for the two weeks training. We have a mockup of the Nazi facility where you will reside. You will be trained on how officers eat, shower, sleep, and everything in between."

Tossing his swagger stick onto the table, the general looked up and asked, "Any questions?"

Overwhelmed by the sudden turn of events, and

not even knowing what questions to ask, both men shook their heads. "Good!" the general exclaimed.

Wagner held up a hand, "Pardon me, I do have one question, sir."

Wagner and Becker were both stunned and jumped when the general shouted, "Sprechen sie Deutsch!"

Wagner flushed and looked sheepish for having been scolded for forgetting the instruction to speak only German.

The general good-naturedly tapped Wagner's shoulder with his swagger stick. "That was a test. Just remember, your very lives depend on speaking German exclusively. Now, what was your question?"

Having recovered from his *faux pas*, Wagner asked in perfect German, "Provided we survive this *mission,* how are we to be extracted after we blow hell outta the place?"

"Ah, well… we're working on that," the general replied in German. It was apparent that he was unsure of the method of rescue.

• • •

After their briefing by General Rochester, Wagner and Becker were whisked to the outskirts of the military base where their training began. Their daily routine consisted of morning runs and calisthenics to stay in top physical shape. Brushing up on German occupied most of their free time, which was sparse. They were also given a crash course on the use of explosives.

Studying the explosives, Wagner said, "Much more sophisticated than the sticks of dynamite we used in the coal mines."

Yes," their instructor who spoke fluent German agreed. "We've come a long way and keep finding more efficient means to eliminate our enemies."

Wagner, looking perplexed, said, "Don't know why I'm considered an explosive expert. I'm far from being an expert at anything, much less explosives. I don't think I'm qualified—"

"Private, you're in the Army now! Here, we don't call the prepared, we prepare the called. Now, stand down and pay attention," the instructor barked.

Wagner shrank back. "Yes, sir," he said.

• • •

The trainees' meals were served in a private dining room overseen by Specialist Hans Snyder, a chef who apparently enjoyed an abundance of his own cooking. Speaking in German, Snyder educated them on proper German etiquette and cuisine. He instructed them on proper terminology for table settings and how the Germans used their utensils. "German officers are expected to act like refined gentlemen," Snyder said, "Never let your guard down and always mind your manners.

"Be mindful that an old German trick is to issue a command in English. If they're suspicious, someone may shout a warning like, "Look out!" just to see who reacts. Be vigilant and never respond to English commands."

• • •

At the end of each day, too exhausted to converse, Wagner and Becker collapsed on their cots and were soon sound asleep.

The same routine was repeated every day for two weeks. After two weeks, Wagner and Becker were deemed ready to proceed with their mission. General Rochester had them brought to his office.

"Gentlemen," the general began in German, "congratulations. I've been informed you're ready to proceed with *Operation Juggernaut*."

"*Operation Juggernaut*?" Becker asked and squinted as he looked over at Wagner.

Wagner just shrugged.

Noticing the confusion on their faces, General Rochester said, "Yes. That's the code name assigned to your mission. Juggernaut is defined as merciless, destructive, and unstoppable," the general said with pride in his voice. "That's what we expect this operation to be, merciless, destructive, and unstoppable.

"Shadow will continue to be our go-between. Tomorrow, you will be transported to Ravensnest, your German base, and then moved to your quarters on site as soon as possible." After a brief pause, the general once again asked, "Any questions?"

Only a thousand, starting with the extraction plan, Wagner thought but didn't dare ask. Once again, both men shook their heads.

"Good!" the general exclaimed. Apparently satisfied he had explained the mission thoroughly, he abruptly stood and extended his hand. Shaking both their hands, he said, "I'm proud of the way the two of you handled yourselves. I know you'll prevail. Godspeed." He then saluted them. Wagner and Becker returned the salute and headed for the door.

• • •

Back in their barracks, Becker said, "Sprechen sie Deutsch! Screw 'em. I think I'm going to be sick. We're just PFCs. How in hell's name did we get into this jaggernut shit?"

"It's juggernaut shit for your information." Wagner responded. "You know the drill. When they asked for volunteers, everyone else was smart enough to step back."

"Yeah! Have that chiseled on my headstone," Becker moaned. "And don't forget to have it inscribed *auf Deutsch* in case I'll be court martialed posthumously."

• • •

Much to Wagner's and Becker's delight, dinner that evening consisted of hamburgers and French fries.

"Hey, Snyder," Wagner said, as he bit into the juicy burger, "what's this?"

"A surprise American farewell dinner. I heard you're leaving tomorrow."

"Farewell dinner? I've heard that out on Alcatraz, they say 'the condemned ate a hearty meal' just before pulling the lever," Becker said, stuffing a wad of French fries into his mouth.

"Ha! You joke about the meal. Does that mean you don't want the apple pie?" Snyder asked, trying to look dejected.

"Hell, no! Bring it on," Becker said and smiled. "I was just yanking your chain. We appreciate your talents and enjoyed our meals. You are the master chef!" *Like I would know a chef from a cook*.

"Thank you," Snyder said. "For that, you get a scoop of ice cream on the pie." Then looking more serious, he added, "Good luck and Godspeed."

Damnit! Even the chef knows we're doomed, Becker thought and continued eating.

Chapter Three

Infiltration

The next morning Corporal Manning appeared carrying two garment bags. Checking the nametags on the hangers, he handed one to Wagner and the other to Becker. He then handed each of them an empty paper bag. "Take off all your clothes and put them and your other personal items in these bags. They will be stored here for you. German-made underwear is included in your new wardrobe. Leave nothing on your person that can be construed as American," Manning, pointing to the garment bags, continued, "Try on your new uniforms while I take your personal items to the exchange where they'll be secured until you return. I'll be back in twenty minutes."

As soon as Manning left, Wagner took the new uniform out of the garment bag and emitted a low whistle. "This is some set of threads," he grunted as he began to dress.

Becker followed suit. When they were completely dressed in their new uniforms, Wagner put on his officer's service cap and asked Becker, "How do I look?"

"You'd scare the hell outta me," Becker replied as he donned his officer's cap. "Go look in the mirror," he said pointing to the head, "and see for yourself."

Both men stood before the mirrors in the head admiring the transformation. "Think we can pull it off?" Wagner asked. Becker just grinned.

Their admiration of themselves was interrupted when Corporal Manning returned. Wagner and Becker joined him in the main area of the barracks. "Mein Gott!" Manning exclaimed. "If I didn't know better…" He then handed each of the men a pistol complete with leather holster. "No officer worth his salt would be caught without his trusty sidearm." As the men inspected the weapons, including combat knives, Manning added, "Careful, the guns are loaded."

• • •

With the war in full swing, it would've been impossible to fly into Germany. Wagner and Becker were flown to a friendly privately owned airfield in Poland close to the German border. From there they traveled by train to within 150 miles of their destination. They were met at the train station by members of the underground and were transported in an official-looking vehicle supplied by Allies disguised as Nazis to the mountain lair that was close to their target. The entire trip took three days.

When they arrived at their destination, having had the groundwork laid before their arrival, they were taken to the officers' quarters and shown to their room. The private that escorted them announced that the officer's mess was at 7:00 p.m. He then frowned as he looked at their uniforms.

"Pardon me, sirs, but your uniforms…" the private said.

"Ja! We know but…" Wagner responded, brushing at the dust that had accumulated on his jacket.

"Let me take them. I will clean and return them to you before seven."

Wagner shrugged and began to undress. Seeing no reason not to, Becker did likewise. As soon as the private left, Becker started to say something. Wagner put his finger to his lips and pointed to the ceiling. Becker nodded.

"I think I'll shave and get cleaned up," Wagner said, all the while speaking German, and started for the bathroom. After turning the water on full blast, he motioned Becker into the bathroom. Speaking softly, knowing the noise of the running water would drown out their conversation, said, "I think they want to check our uniforms to ensure we're not hiding something." Becker nodded. "They'll probably go over our room with a fine-tooth comb when we're at dinner," Wagner whispered. Even in private the two spoke in German.

Both men had bathed and shaved by the time the private returned with their uniforms.

"Here you are, sirs," he said and hung the uniforms in the armoire.

"Thank you, Private," Wagner said and walked him to the door. "It's still early. Is there someplace we can get a drink before dinner?"

"Why, yes. Fritz's is right next door. It's a small *die mensa*," the private responded with a smile.

Closing the door as soon as the private left, Wagner shook his head when Becker mouthed the question, "Shadow?"

• • •

Wagner looked at his new German watch. "Since we have an hour before dinner, let's check out Fritz's."

When the pair entered Fritz's, they were amazed at the number of German military present. The bar was noisy and smoke-filled. The atmosphere was relaxed and loud laughter filled the air as the patrons joked with each other.

As Wagner and Becker stood in the entrance surveying the room looking for a place to sit, a pretty, young woman approached them. She was dressed in a high-waisted skirt with a tight-fitting bodice, the local waitress garb known as a dirndl. The costume accentuated her ample attributes which didn't go unnoticed by Wagner or Becker. She smiled at them and pointed to a small table at the rear of the bar. Wagner nodded. As they snaked their way through the crowded bar, Dieter, a very drunk patron, approached from behind and slipped his arm around the waitress' waist.

"Come on, *Liebchen*. Dance with me," Dieter slurred.

Pushing the patron away, the waitress wiggled free from his grasp. "Not now. Maybe later," she scolded as she adjusted her dress.

The drunk winked and staggered off toward the bar.

After Wagner and Becker were seated, the waitress asked for their drink orders. Wagner couldn't take his eyes off her. When he finally realized she was waiting for their order, he was embarrassed by what he was thinking and said, "Zwei Bier!" He then pointed to Becker and himself.

When the waitress left, Wagner followed her with his eyes. He then whispered to Becker, "This mission may not be as bad as we thought."

Becker just rolled his eyes in disgust.

Their beer was served in frosted, thick glass

beer mugs. When the waitress set them down on the table, she slid one closer to Wagner. Confused, he looked up and she tilted her head toward the mug. Taking the hint, Wagner slowly turned the mug, closely examining it. The word *Shadow* was etched in the frost on the outside of the glass. *Shadow? She's Shadow, our contact?* He immediately put his hand around the mug obliterating the word and smiled up at the waitress. "What's your name?" he asked.

"Lina," she replied, "Lina Zimmer."

Wagner handed her some Deutsche marks that included a generous tip.

"Thank you," Lina said then added, "I work here every night." She then turned and left the table.

When she was out of earshot, a bewildered Becker asked, "What was that all about?"

"Lina is Shadow," Wagner whispered.

Becker coughed as he choked on his beer.

• • •

Wagner glanced at his watch. It was 6:45. "Drink up, it's time to leave," he said. "Don't want to be late for dinner and draw attention to ourselves."

Becker stood and led the way. Wagner looked around for Lina as they wormed their way through the bar. All the bar stools were occupied, as well as many of the tables. It appeared that Fritz's was a popular after-work watering hole. Blue collar workers mingled with men in business suits and military uniforms. The room was filled with chatter and loud laughter. Other than the waitresses, very few other women were in the bar. Much to Wagner's disappointment, Lina was nowhere to be seen.

• • •

The officer's dining room was in their hotel so they didn't have far to go. Several officers were already seated when Wagner and Becker entered the dining room. They were greeted by a maître d' who escorted them to their table. When they approached, the two officers who were already seated stood. After the maître d' retreated, introductions were made.

"*Wilkommen*!" one of the officers said as he greeted the newcomers. Pointing to his companion, he said, "This is Captain Schultz and I am Captain Fischer."

Remembering their lessons before leaving the States, Wagner recalled that they were expected to shake hands. Their instructor told them that the Germans were the world's greatest hand shakers, and usually shook upon greeting and again upon departing.

Extending his hand, Wagner said, "Captain

Wagner. A pleasure to meet you." Then he introduced Becker. Once the all-around hand shaking was completed, the four officers sat and the maître d' brought a bottle of wine and poured four glasses.

Fischer stood again, and holding his wine glass high, he offered a toast. "Here's to the *Vaterland*," he said with exuberance in his voice.

The other three stood, and the four officers clicked and drained their glasses.

Dinner conversation was light. It appeared no one wanted to express an opinion on how the war was going. Soon a waitress approached carrying shoulder high a large tray laden with a variety of dishes. Her face was obscured by the number of dishes on the tray. Wagner looked up when the waitress placed a plate before him. It was Lina.

"Well, hello again," he said in a soft voice. "You do get around."

When Lina ignored him, he felt guilty and wondered if he had compromised her cover in any way. It appeared Captain Fischer overheard Wagner's comment. As soon as Lina finished serving and retreated, Fischer said firmly to Wagner, "The wait staff has been instructed not to interact with the officers." Then, watching Lina retreat to the kitchen, he added, "I can't say I blame you for your interest in that one." Wagner was relieved he hadn't put Lina in jeopardy. Next time he would be more circumspect. He smiled at Fischer. Becker, having overheard the conversation, diverted his attention to his dinner. *Wagner is gonna get us killed.*

• • •

After dinner, when Wagner and Becker were alone in their room, Becker looked sternly at Wagner. He didn't need to say anything. Judging by the look on his face, Wagner knew his flirting with Lina could've put them all in peril. He took Becker's hand and fake wrote the word, "*Sorry*" on the back of Becker's hand. Becker stared at his hand suddenly realizing, just like Helen Keller, they had a way to communicate. He grinned and took Wagner's hand and finger wrote, "OK."

• • •

As they were preparing to go to bed, they were surprised by a light tap on their door. Becker put his finger to his lips and went to the door. When he opened it a crack, he saw Lina standing in the corridor nervously looking around. Opening the door wider, he beckoned her inside.

Once inside, Lina fumbled in her apron pocket and produced a small note. She was also aware the room could be bugged so she didn't speak. Thinking the note might be an invitation, Becker took it and handed it to Wagner. After reading it, Wagner handed it back to Becker indicating for him to read it. The note said, "Meet me at 2:00 a.m. tomorrow behind Fritz's." Both men nodded. Lina took the note, opened the door, and peered out into the corridor. Then she slipped out of the room and was gone like a shadow.

· · ·

The next night, Wagner and Becker stood in the dark alley behind Fritz's nervously waiting for Lina. They both jumped when the rear door to Fritz's opened, but breathed a sigh of relief when Lina stepped out and closed the door. She was carrying a bundle.

"I'm sorry I startled you. I just closed the bar," Lina said. Moving closer to the men she continued in a soft voice. "I've been instructed to familiarize you with your target. I'll pack a lunch and later today I'll pick you up. We'll drive to the mountain. I know a nice place for a picnic that overlooks your target. I also have drawn a map of the area and will bring it with me." Then handing the bundle to Wagner, she said, "This is more appropriate wear for the mountains, ski pants and sweaters. Meet me in front of the hotel at noon."

Accepting the bundle, Wagner asked, "You won't be in any danger, will you?" Concern evident in his voice.

"No, at least not more than usual." Then glancing over her shoulder, Lina said, "It's too dangerous to stay here out in the open. You go back to the hotel. I'll make sure the bar is secure and go out through the front."

The men immediately left and Lina watched until she could no longer see them. She then turned back toward the rear door. When she put her hand on the doorknob, Dieter emerged from the shadows.

"What are you up to?" Dieter demanded.

Fear gripped Lina. She replied, "What? Why, nothing. I just…"

"Never mind. I heard everything. So, you're too good to dance with me…I'll show you!" Dieter slurred.

"Ah, come on, Dieter. I was just trying to…" Lina started but Dieter cut her off.

"Sounds to me like you and your friends are spies," Dieter grumbled and swayed apparently having trouble standing.

Realizing she had been caught, and even in Dieter's drunken stupor, the Nazis would probably investigate his claims. Lina's mind raced for a solution. Knowing Dieter was attracted to her, and trying to buy time, she cooed, "Don't be jealous. Come on in and I'll make it up to you."

"And just how you going to do that?"

"Come on and I'll show you," Lina answered.

"*Gut*, but no tricks."

"No tricks, I promise," Lina said.

Back inside the bar, Lina pointed to a table. "You take a seat and I'll mix us a drink."

Except for one overhead night light, the bar was dark and Dieter squinted trying to get oriented. "Can we have some light?" he asked.

"Not unless you want to draw attention to us being here," Lina said as she mixed the drinks.

Two years ago, when Lina was recruited to help the Allies, she was given a cyanide pill. Knowing how cruel the Germans could be, the choice was to take the cyanide rather than be tortured in case she was captured. She kept it with her at all times secured in a heart-shaped locket she wore around her neck.

Lina had never killed before, but rationalized it was a necessary evil. Knowing if Dieter lived, he would expose not only her, but Wagner and Becker and they would all be tortured and killed. Lina made her decision. It was either him or them. She extracted the pill from the locket. Pausing a few moments, she once again weighed her options. Finally, deciding the three were more important to the cause than Dieter, she dropped the cyanide into

Dieter's drink and stirred until it dissolved. *God forgive me.*

Approaching the table where Dieter sat, Lina's hands shook as she sat the drinks down.

"It's about damn time," Dieter slurred and eyed her suspiciously.

Fearing she was losing his trust; she began to unbutton her blouse, exposing ample cleavage.

"Now where were we?" she asked in a sultry voice as she saluted him with her drink.

Drunk and dazed by the sudden turn of events, Dieter stared at Lina's exposed breast and absentmindedly picked up his glass. When he raised it to his lips, Lina raised her glass and took a large swallow. Dieter did likewise.

Lina knew it took approximately three minutes to die after taking cyanide. She carefully watched Dieter as he struggled with the poison. Taking his glass from his hand before he could spill the remainer of its contents, she watched as he tried to formulate words but nothing came out. When his head finally fell with a thud face down on the table, guilt assaulted her, but considering the alternative, she felt she had no other recourse.

Wringing her hands in despair, Lina waited for a few minutes to collect her thoughts. When she was sure Dieter was dead, she washed the glasses and set a bottle of whiskey in front of him. She did this because she had no feasible way to remove the body and hoped when it was discovered, his demise would be attributed to his alcoholism. From her training, she knew there were no outward signs of cyanide poising and she doubted there would be an autopsy since Dieter was a nobody and known to be a drunk. If asked by the police, she could say he must've been hiding in the men's room. She had not checked there before locking up.

$$\bullet\ \bullet\ \bullet$$

After a sleepless night, Lina arose early and packed lunch for the trip to the mountain. She had arranged to borrow a vehicle from Olga, a friend. Upon arrival at Olga's flat to pick up the car, Olga asked, "Oh, Lina, haven't you heard?"

Lina was once again gripped with fear. "Heard what?" she exclaimed.

"Why, when Fritz opened the bar this morning, he found Dieter dead."

"What?" Lina faked surprise.

"Yes, dead inside the bar.. I heard since you closed up last night, the authorities want to question you"

Oh, no! "I didn't see Dieter when I closed," Lina said. Then thinking it may be to her advantage, she added, "I'll go straight to the police and answer their questions."

"I'll go with you," Olga offered. Before Lina could object, Olga grabbed her purse and headed for the door.

Lina knew Olga was a busybody and always wanted to be the first to spread the news—good or bad—preferably bad. However, having a friend for support was appealing, so Lina didn't object. When they arrived at police headquarters, Lina was taken into an interrogation room. Much to Olga's chagrin, she was required to stay in the visitor's waiting room.

Sgt. Karl Müller escorted Lina to the interrogation room and took a seat at the table across from her. "Would you state your full name for the record," he said. It was a command, not a question.

"Lina Zimmer."

Writing on a form, Müller didn't look up when he asked, "Date of birth?"

"October 5, 1920."

"Were you at Fritz's bar last night?"

"Yes."

"When did you leave?" Müller asked.

"I closed the bar and left around two. The bar was empty when I left."

"So, you didn't see the deceased, Dieter

Newmann, in the bar area?"

"No."

"Did you check the men's room before closing?"

"No." Lina replied.

"Did you see anyone lurking around outside?" Müller asked.

"No."

"And the doors were locked when you left?"

"Yes."

Müller paused and examined the form. "When did you last see the deceased, Deiter Newmann?"

"We were so busy, I really don't remember seeing him."

"Were the two of you friends?" Müller asked.

"No, I just knew him as a patron," Lina responded. *Where's this going?*

Müller tapped his pen on the form as he studied it. After a few moments, and apparently not having any more questions for Lina, he said, "That's all for now. You're free to go." As he placed his fountain pen in his shirt pocket, he added, "We may have more questions later."

Lina nodded. "Thank you," she replied and stood. She paused, and knowing it may attract more attention to her, she couldn't help but ask, "How did Mr. Newmann die?"

"Since there was no evidence of foul play, it

appears he finally drank himself to death. He must've found a place to hide, and after the bar closed and being alone in the bar, was like a fox in a henhouse. A critical piece of evidence was the open bottle of whiskey."

Müller stood and said, "Thank you for coming in." He took her arm and walked Lina back out to the waiting room.

Olga put the magazine she had been browsing aside when Lina approached. "That was quick," she said as she stood.

"I didn't have much to tell them," Lina said, hoping Olga would abort bombarding her with questions.

"What kind of questions did they ask?" Olga persisted.

"Personal information, name, age, address, and how I knew Dieter."

Disappointment evident in her voice, Olga said, "Oh, is that all?"

"Yes."

"Did they say how Dieter died?" Olga asked.

"No."

"What do you think happened?" Olga asked on the way back to her apartment.

"I couldn't say. Maybe his heart gave out from all the drinking."

Olga pulled to the curb in front of her residence. "You go ahead and take the car. I have some calls to make," she said.

I'll just bet you do. "Thanks again," Lina said as she slid over to the driver's side.

Chapter Four

Observation

Wagner and Becker were waiting for Lina in front of the hotel when she drove up. They were dressed in the ski pants and sweaters she provided the night before. As soon as they got into the car, Wagner noticed something was wrong with Lina. Looking at her, he asked, "What happened?"

"I'll tell you later," she said and directed her attention to driving.

No one spoke the entire trip to the mountain. After they arrived and spread the picnic in a park, Wagner said, "Okay, it's later. Now tell us what happened."

Lina couldn't hold back the tears as she related to them how she killed Dieter and was interrogated by the authorities.

Taking Lina's hand, Wagner said, "Lina, you had no choice. Dieter would have spilled to the Nazis what he saw and heard and we would all be tortured and eventually killed."

Becker chimed in. "That's right. By killing one man you most likely saved hundreds, maybe thousands of lives by protecting us and allowing us to do our job. Don't lose sight of the fact that we're fighting for freedom and most of the time when we kill, we have no choice. We must act on the situations as they are presented to us. We don't have the luxury of having time to analyze the results."

Lina, dabbing at her eyes, said, "Thank you for putting things in prospective. I didn't think of it like that. I'll get over it in time, and I'm sorry to have burdened you with my weakness."

"You didn't burden us," Becker said. "We're here to help each other."

Lina bit her lower lip. "What if something comes of the fact Dieter didn't have an open bottle…?" she asked. "How do I explain that?"

"You don't have to explain it. The less you say, the better off you'll be," Wagner responded. "Besides, your story is that you weren't there so you don't know what Dieter was doing."

Lina nodded. "Thank you for your support," she whispered as she dried her eyes. Eager to change the subject, Lina turned her attention to unwrapping sandwiches. "After lunch," she said, "we'll take a short walk and I'll show you the target."

• • •

Looking like picknickers, they walked around the park. Lina pointed out places of interest. "There at the base of the mountain," she said, "is the target tunnel. Here, take the binoculars. You can see the entrance from here. It extends approximately half a mile through the mountain. The Nazis did some finish work on the inside and even strung lights along the top of the tunnel."

"That was considerate." Since he was deemed to be the explosive expert, still surveying with the binoculars, Wagner asked, "Where do they store the explosives?"

"Look to the left of the entrance. There's a small shack. That's where the dynamite is stored." After a pause, Lina added, "It's not used much since the tunnel has been completed."

Handing the binoculars to Becker, Wagner continued to stare at the shack. "Hope there's enough left to do the job," he mused.

"Wonder how we can get a closer look?" Becker asked.

After a moment, Lina blurted, "Use your rank! Disguised as captains, you're here to inspect the tunnel. Tomorrow, procure a car and driver, and go to the Needles under the guise of conducting an inspection."

Looking sheepish, Wagner said, "Why didn't I think of that."

"It's tough going from a PFC to captain overnight," Becker said with a grin. "Let's do it.

The sooner we get this job finished, the better. I'm eager to get outta here."

"Which reminds me," Wagner said. Looking at Lina, he asked, "Do you know what our extraction plan is after we blow hell outta this place?"

Lina shook her head. "I've not been included in the details."

"Hmm," Wagner mused. "I have a funny feeling we may be on our own, Becker."

Becker shrugged. "Not surprising," he murmured.

Lina took Wagner's arm and turned him toward her. "Take me with you," she pleaded.

"What?" Wagner stammered and looked at Becker. Becker just raised his brow. "If we can," Wagner said and patted Lina's hand to reassure her. *Not even sure we'll be able to get out alive.*

• • •

The next morning over breakfast in the officer's mess, Wagner asked the other officers seated at their table how he could obtain a car and driver. One of the officers said, "Ask the captain in charge, his name is Klaus." Then pointing across the room, added, "That's him seated at the head table doing all the talking."

"Thank you," Wagner said and looked at the head table where Klaus was seated. Klaus seemed to be engaged in a serious conversation with his tablemates. Studying the middle aged, overweight, balding German, Wagner thought that he had the air of a playground bully, a jackass who was accustomed to using his rank to strike fear into the hearts of his fellow men.

Placing his napkin on the table, Wagner cringed. Knowing you live or die by your choices, he threw caution to the wind and stood. Straightening his shoulders, he adjusted his uniform jacket, and boldly walked toward the head table. Becker watched Wagner's every move with trepidation. Knowing Wagner as well as he did, Becker was apprehensive as to what might transpire. He was on pins and needles as he watched.

Wagner approached the head table, cleared his throat, and addressed Captain Klaus. "Pardon me for interrupting, Captain, but I was told you could arrange a car and driver."

"Yes, I can, but just what do you need a car for?" Klaus asked not even looking up from his plate.

Wagner was irritated at the apparent insult. "We're here to conduct an inspection of the passage through the Needles," Wagner said with authority. "Captain Becker and I are expected to submit a report by the end of the week."

"Hmm, first I've heard of it," Klaus muttered

as he smeared butter onto a biscuit. "Who sent you?" The impact of the interruption was evident. Klaus held his hand up to quiet those engaged in conversation. After all, he was in charge!

It's now or never! "That's confidential! What gives you the right to question me?" Wagner banged his fist on the table and leaned forward just inches from Klaus's face. Silver service clattered to the floor, juice glasses overturned, and coffee sloshed onto the tablecloth. "Do you want me to report your unwillingness to cooperate?" The conversation was loud and the entire officers' mess fell silent as those in attendance turned their attention to the head table.

Turning red, from rage or embarrassment, or both, Klaus stammered, "Ah, why no! I meant no disrespect." It was apparent Klaus had never been challenged and didn't know how to deal with it. "Of course, I can arrange a car and driver. I'll have them here within the hour."

"Thank you. I'll report your cooperation," Wagner said. Still leaning a few inches from Klaus's face, he gave him a final stare. He then turned and went back to his table. He felt Klaus's eyes burning holes in his back as he crossed the room. *Looks like I've made a powerful enemy.*

As soon as Wagner sat down, Becker whispered,

"You're playing Russian roulette with five live rounds in the gun, not just one. You realize we're standing on the threshold of eternity and we may not live long enough to finish our mission."

Still fighting with his anger, Wagner ignored the reprimand. The show of strength and courage provided the much-needed resolve. The encounter with Klaus was gripping and he defeated the giant. This encounter was really the first time he knew he was up to the task.

Their tablemates, Fischer and Schultz, remained noncommittal. It appeared to Becker they were afraid for their lives by merely being tablemates with Wagner.

• • •

After finishing their breakfast, Wagner and Becker left the dining room. When they stepped outside, they found a military vehicle standing at the curb. The driver came around the front of the car and opened the door. "Captain Klaus instructed me to drive you to wherever you want to go," he said.

Feeling smug at having won the battle, Wagner looked at Becker and whispered, "Now that's what I call service."

Still stinging from Wagner's heart-stopping encounter with Klaus, Becker retorted, "I think it comes with a price. One you may not want to pay."

As far as he was concerned, if Becker had his way, they'd be hitching their way to their destination.

When they were secure inside the car, Wagner said to the driver, "Take us to the Needles."

"Yes, sir," the driver replied.

Becker paid closer attention to the route the driver took in case they ever had to make the trip on their own. When they arrived, they were taken by an armed guard to a small building situated close to the entrance of the tunnel. "This is Captain Bauer's office," the driver said.

"Wait for us while we conduct our inspection," Becker ordered as they exited the car.

Still high from having won the stare-down with Klaus, Wagner didn't knock. He opened the door to the captain's office and strutted in. The man seated behind the desk looked up, surprise evident on his face. The name plate on the desk identified the commander as Captain Bauer.

Before Bauer could speak, Wagner said, "Good morning, Captain. I'm Captain Wagner and this is Captain Becker. As you may know, we're explosive experts here on strict orders from *der Führer* to conduct an inspection of the passage through the Needles."

The expression on the captain's face went from surprise to displeasure. It was evident he was insulted by Wagner and Becker just walking in without knocking. However, when he heard they were there under strict orders from *der Führer,* although he wasn't aware of any such orders, he didn't challenge them. *Why wasn't I informed of this inspection?* he thought.

"Yes, of course. I've been expecting you," he lied, and indicated for them to take a seat. After they were seated, Bauer continued to lie, "I have a team ready to guide you through the tunnel and answer your questions." He managed a contrived smile.

It was obvious Bauer was lying. "You were expecting us? That's odd. This was supposed to be a surprise visit," Wagner said and frowned.

Bauer began to sweat. It must've dawned on him the reason why he wasn't informed. "Ah, yes. Well, you see," he stuttered, "we're always ready for an inspection. It's just good practice to be prepared—"

"I see!" Wagner interrupted. "Enough excuses. Can we get started immediately?"

"Of course, I'll send for your guide. Excuse me for a moment." Bauer rushed out of the office and ordered the private standing guard to summon Herr Steiner. Wagner and Becker heard him instruct the guard to tell Steiner an inspection team was on site.

Becker couldn't help himself. "So, we live to

fight another day, no thanks to you," he whispered.

Wagner was now in the habit of ignoring Becker's reprimands.

• • •

A few moments later, one of the civilian engineers, Herman Steiner, knocked on Bauer's door. After introductions were made, Bauer instructed Steiner to escort Wagner and Becker through the tunnel. Judging by the look on Steiner's face, it was apparent he was mystified by the request.

Before Steiner could say anything, Bauer blurted, "This is the inspection team we've been expecting."

Picking up on the play, Steiner replied, "Oh, yes. Of course." Then to Wagner and Becker, he said, "Come with me." and he led them to the entrance of the tunnel.

• • •

Wagner, being familiar with mine shafts by having worked in a coalmine in West Virginia, noticed the shaft was reinforced with concrete rather than timber.

"Herr Steiner, why did you use concrete for support rather than timber?" Wagner asked. Although he knew the answer, he didn't want to appear to be too knowledgeable and thereby raise suspicion.

Adjusting his glasses, Steiner replied, "Ah, well, because, in this area, the ground tends to shift. We thought concrete would be more stable."

"I see." Still pretending to be a novice, Wagner asked, "What kind of explosives did you use to widen the corridor?"

Steiner looked at Wagner with disbelief. *This is supposed to be an explosives expert?* Apparently, recovering from the shock, Steiner answered, "Gunpowder and dynamite were used for the blasting."

"I see. Gunpowder *and* dynamite!" Wagner said. Obviously, still playing the fool, he looped his thumbs over his belt and looking around, asked, "Where do you store it?"

"In that shed over there," Steiner said, pointing to a small building. *Where does the Reich get idiots like this one?*

"Hmm, since this is an all-inclusive report to headquarters, may I examine the storage facility? You understand the command wants to ensure the troops are safe," Wagner said. Becker just looked at him in disbelief. *Make that six live rounds in the gun.*

"Yes, of course," Steiner said, but couldn't disguise the contempt in his voice. *What gives this young twerp the right to challenge my safety practices?*

• • •

Taking a few minutes to do what he hoped looked like was an official inspection, Wagner was elated when he noticed a number kegs of gunpowder stacked in the corner of the storage shed. *That's all we need.*

When they left the shed, he said to Steiner, "Looks like you've taken every precaution to be safe with the explosives. Rest assured that my report will reflect that." Then, taking a quick look around, "In fact, overall, you've done an excellent job."

"Why, thank you, Captain," Steiner said, relief evident in his voice.

Returning to their car, still imitating an air of importance, Wagner opted not to bother to report back to Captain Bauer. He just ordered the driver to return them to their hotel. It appeared to Becker that Wagner was enjoying the disrespect he was heaping on the German command. *Bad idea!* Becker can visualize where Wagner's hubris will ultimately lead them.

• • •

When they arrived back at the hotel, Wagner suggested they take a walk around the downtown plaza and view the sights.

"Excellent idea," Becker said. "I need to stretch my legs."

Their journey took them to the town square. A large fountain was positioned in the center. It was adorned with sculptures of German soldiers. Water splashing into a pool at the base of the fountain provided enough noise to make it difficult for anyone in the vicinity to overhear their conversation. Selecting a section of the fountain that was isolated, Wagner stood with a foot propped on the edge of the two-foot concrete wall surrounding the pool. Placing his elbow on his bent knee, Wagner leaned forward and whispered, "We hit the jackpot. Everything we need is in the storage shed."

Taking advantage of a situation where they could talk freely, Becker replied, "Wonderful!" Now, how do we proceed?" There was no room for error. One miscalculation could be the end of both of them.

"Elementary, my dear Watson," Wagner replied. "We commandeer a vehicle and make a late-night visit to the Needles. We transport as many kegs of gunpowder as is necessary midway into the tunnel and trail a line of gunpowder to the Austrian side. As soon as we're out of the tunnel, we light the gunpowder and dynamite and run like hell."

"Sounds easy enough. How many times have you done this?" Becker asked, thinking of the consequences in the event something went wrong and they were swallowed up in the collapse with no means of escape. And what plan did Wagner have in the event they were caught in the act?

"Well, personally, none. But I've seen it done several times in the coal mines."

"That's comforting," Becker mused.

"Ah, come on! It'll be fun," Wagner teased, knowing full-well they had less than a fifty-fifty chance of succeeding, much less surviving.

Chapter Five

Preparation

Lina lived with her parents on the family farm outside of Innsbruck, a small town in Austria that was controlled by Germany. Their farm was situated close to the Bavarian Alps. Lina hiked the mountains in the summer and skied in the winter. She spent so much time exploring the mountains that she knew the area surrounding her home well enough that she never got lost. She could find her way home, even in the dark.

The Zimmers' ancestors homesteaded the farm. It was handed down from generation to generation. Now in her early teens, Lina, the only child of Ludwig and Gretchen Zimmer, was cherished by her parents. They were happy and comfortable in the farmhouse that had been built by Ludwig's ancestors. Although small, the house was alive with the memories of those who lived there before. Ludwig relished telling Lina stories about her ancestry. His memory was sharp and the pride in his voice was unmistakable as he regaled her with family history. Lina became acquainted with her grandparents and great grandparents through Ludwig's story telling.

The Zimmers' farm was self-sufficient and met their needs. They had a milk cow, chickens, a large garden, and fruit trees. Gretchen harvested the produce and canned what they could not consume. She dried apples and berries and stored her canned fruits and vegetables in a root cellar near the house. Their closest neighbor raised cattle and would trade beef for fresh vegetables and eggs. Gretchen cut the beef into strips and made enough jerky to last through the winter. The only time the Zimmers went into town was on Sunday to worship. They were devout Catholics and were liked and respected by friends and neighbors.

• • •

Week after week when they attended church, the Zimmers heard rumors of how the Jews were being treated. They were horrified when they heard the Jews were taken to concentration camps. There, they were used in experiments, starved, beaten, and worked as slaves before eventually being killed in cruel and inhuman ways. When Hitler's new party rose to power, the Zimmers resisted. Unable to accept the horror of the Jewish fate, Ludwig was outspoken and expressed to confidents his concern over the future of Austria under the Third Reich. It wasn't long before Ludwig's comments reached the ears of the Nazi command.

Colonel Boris Ackermann was Hitler's appointed mayor of Innsbruck. He was ruthless in his administration of *justice*. No one dared challenge him for fear of being sent to the camps. Even non-Jewish dissidents were sent to the camps to keep them from speaking against the Reich. When rumors reached Ackermann that Ludwig had been stirring up resistance, he went berserk. "We cannot allow an insurrection!" Ackermann barked. "Bring the Zimmers to me at once."

• • •

A truck was immediately dispatched to the Zimmers' farm and all three Zimmers were taken to German headquarters, in Garmisch-Partenkirchen, Germany, a mere forty miles from Innsbruck. The two soldiers who were sent to make the arrest were hostile to the Zimmers, roughly pushing them into the bed of the truck. Half scared out of her wits, Lina huddled close to her mother. Gretchen held Lina close in her arms. Although she, too, was gripped with fear, she whispered in Lina's ear, "Remember, we're in God's hands. He'll take care of us. Everything's going to be alright." However, Gretchen's manner varied from the tone of her voice. It was obvious that Gretchen, too, anticipated the worse.

When they reached Garmisch-Partenkirchen,

Lina was separated from her parents. A matron appeared as soon as the truck stopped a Nazi headquarters. She had apparently been waiting for them and she immediately took charge of Lina and urged her toward a building across from Nazi headquarters. When Lina jerked her arm free from the matron's grasp to look back to see where her parents were being taken, she stumbled and fell. She cried out, "Mother!"

Seeing her daughter fall and feeling her daughter's distress, Gretchen put a fist to her lips to stifle a sob. She, too, knew their future was tentative. *Will I ever see her again?*

Lina, of course, didn't understand exactly what was transpiring and fear gripped her. She obviously knew something terrible was happening.

• • •

Ludwig and Gretchen Zimmer were immediately hustled into a sterile interrogation room inside Nazi headquarters. Their captors made them wait almost an hour before they were brought before an authority for questioning. Now, standing side by side before Burgermeister Ackermann, they were harshly interrogated and denigrated.

When questioned, Ludwig readily and truthfully admitted he disagreed with the war and the direction Germany was headed. Ludwig believed that, by telling the truth, justice would prevail. However, at the time he testified, he didn't realize he was sealing *their* fate, his and Gretchen's.

"Herr Zimmer," Ackermann snarled, "what authority do you have to criticize the Nazi command?"

"The only justification I have is being a citizen of Austria. I think that in and of itself gives me the right to question the fate of my country."

Ackermann was not used to arrestees being so bold and articulate. He didn't like it and sneered at Ludwig, "Your actions are tantamount to insurrection against the state punishable by imprisonment or death. Do you still want to proceed down that path?"

Ludwig blanched. *Imprisonment or death.* He hesitated before answering and glanced at Gretchen. When he saw the look on her face, he started to back down for her sake. Although she knew she was probably sealing their death warrants, Gretchen took his hand and shook her head. She, too, was a proud Austrian. Ludwig, realizing Gretchen opposed his surrender, pulled himself up to his six-foot height and took a deep breath.

"Yes," he said in a firm voice. "I will not disgrace family nor my ancestors by caving in to a radical dictator." Gretchen squeezed his hand. She knew what was coming. *What will happen to Lina?*

With Ludwig having confessed, and there being no need to proceed further with the interrogation, Ackermann adjourned the hearing. Having established guilt, sentence was imposed immediately. Ludwig and Gretchen were ordered to be taken to one of the concentration camps. Lina's fate was also sealed and she would become a ward of the state and indoctrinated into the Third Reich. Summoning the military guards stationed outside his office, Ackermann ordered, "Take these two prisoners to Dachau."

The guards saluted and one of them motioned with his rifle for the Zimmers to go ahead of him to the truck which was waiting in the courtyard. Ackermann stopped the other guard before he left the hearing room and whispered to him, "When they try to escape, shoot them." The meaning was clear. They were not to arrive at Dachau alive.

• • •

Lina was told her parents were incarcerated for their political beliefs and would remain in custody until after the war. In the meantime, she would be enrolled in school. When the teachers tried to force the Nazi superior race theory on the students, Lina inwardly resisted. However, after learning her parents had been incarcerated, she knew better than to challenge the Nazi way of thinking. Lina had been home-schooled by her parents, both academically and spiritually and had a good foundation to fall back on. Clinging to the hope that she would someday be reunited with her parents, she went along to get along.

• • •

The older girls at the school were trained in various skills to prepare them for the future. Some were seamstresses. Others were trained as cooks or housekeepers. Lina's good looks and personality were the reason she was trained as a waitress. It was well known that alcohol loosened lips and men liked to brag to pretty women about their exploits. She was given a waitress position in a small town close to the Alps known as Ravensnest. Her main function was to spy for the Reich.

• • •

Lina, now in her twenties, had been working in Ravensnest for three years. One evening, a Nazi soldier entered the bar. Lina thought he looked familiar but couldn't place him. When she approached his table to take his order, he looked up and recognition lit up his face. "Lina!" he exclaimed. "Lina Zimmer!"

"Yes," Lina said, still confused.

"Don't you remember me?" the soldier asked.

"Karl Schmidt."

When Lina didn't show any sign of recognition, he added, "We went to *finishing school* together."

Suddenly it hit her and memories of those years flooded her mind. Disguising her anxiety, she managed a smile and said, "Oh, of course. Finishing school? Is that what you call it?"

They both laughed remembering those harsh days. "Here," Karl said and stood and pulled a chair out, "sit with me."

Lina looked around at the crowded bar. "Sorry, Karl. I'm on duty."

Karl nodded. "When do you get off?" he asked. "Ten."

"May I have the privilege of buying you a late dinner?" Karl asked.

Lina smiled. "Of course. I'd love to catch up with you. Fritz makes a pretty good sandwich. We can eat here if you like."

Karl stood. "Anywhere, as long as it's with you," he said, and offered her his hand.

Lina blushed, and took Karl's hand, "Okay then, meet me here at ten."

• • •

Over dinner consisting mainly of sandwiches and beer, Lina and Karl related to each other how their lives progressed after they finished school.

Karl was immediately inducted into the military. He was stationed in Berlin but was now on his way to his new assignment. He, of course, couldn't tell her where he was going. Everything pertaining to the military was now hush-hush.

Changing the subject, Karl asked, "Do you still ski?"

"No, and haven't for years. I'm afraid I'd break every bone in my body if I tried now."

"Too bad. Thought I'd get some skiing in before heading to my new assignment."

"These mountains are renowned for skiing," Lina said. "I think you'd enjoy the slopes."

Karl reared back in his chair. "That was an excellent dinner. Thank you for suggesting it."

"Fritz is well known in this part of the country," Lina replied. "I think he's Ravensnest's claim to fame."

The couple sat in quiet reflection for a few moments. Finally, Karl took Lina's hand in his. Looking into her eyes, he said, "I was so sorry when I heard about your parents."

"What! Wh…what about my parents?" Lina sputtered.

"Why, you didn't know"?

"Know what!" Lina demanded jerking her hand from his.

Looking around to see if her outburst had been noticed by the other patrons, Karl motioned for Lina to settle down. He finally said, "They never made it to Dachau."

"Oh, no!" Lina gasped. "What happened?" She asked and swiped frantically at the tears that were forming in her eyes.

Karl leaned closer to keep others from overhearing their conversation. "The story I heard was they were shot trying to escape," he said in a soft voice.

Lina hung her head. She was consumed in sorrow. *Trying to escape?* Not likely.

Karl tried to put his arm around her shoulders to comfort her, but she pulled away. Karl shrank back when he saw the look in her eyes. He looked around to see if anyone was showing any interest in them.

"They lied to me," Lina groaned. "They lied to me. They've been lying to me all along, and my parents were dead the whole time." Lina had been told if she cooperated with the Reich, her parents would be safe. Now she was hit head-on with reality, and she knew Karl wouldn't lie about it. *I'll get even with them any way I can. I'll turn the tables on them, the lying bastards.* Standing, Lina said, "It's late, Karl. Thank you for dinner. I must go." She turned and left the bar. Karl stared after her. Distress and disappointment were evident from her posture.

That was the defining moment in Lina's life. She promised herself she'd avenge her parents no matter what. Strength and courage would replace the anguish she felt. It was providential.

• • •

Lina had made many contacts in her position as a waitress at Fritz's. One of her contacts was a freelancer by the name of Albert Koch. Lina knew Albert wasn't loyal to either the Axis or the Allies and worked both sides of the street. It was rumored that he would do anything for a Deutsche mark.

The next time Albert visited the bar, Lina sat down at his table. In a conspiratorial tone, she told him she wanted to help the Allies with the war effort. Albert raised his brow. "Really! What brought that on?" he asked.

"It's personal," she replied. "Will you help me?" she pleaded.

"Absolutely," Albert said. He looked at her and saw the hurt in her eyes. He also knew she had been spying for the Nazis in order to ensure the safety of her parents. He assumed her reason for turning on the Reich must be astronomical. Knowing she didn't have much money, he added, "For you, honey, no charge."

Lina gave Albert a weak smile. "Thank you," she whispered. "How soon can I start?"

"I'll get back to you."

• • •

Albert was successful in lining Lina up with some agents who worked with the Allies. She was checked out and deemed to be perfect for their purposes. She was trusted by the Nazis, she was in a place where the flow of information was abundant, and she obviously had a vengeful lust to burn the Third Reich. Lina had already been trained in the art of spying by the Axis. The Allies gave her a refresher course and the code name *Shadow*. In the event she became exposed as a double agent, the Nazis would show her no mercy, so they provided her with a cyanide pill. Even though they realized she was in a position to gather important information, they hoped her lust for revenge wouldn't be her downfall.

To Lina, her cause was greater than her life. Having suddenly lost all that was dear to her, she wasn't afraid to take chances with her own life. She would exact her perceived pound of flesh. She remembered one of her father's famous sayings: *You can get bitter or you can get even.* Henceforth, that would be her motto.

Chapter Six

Insubordination

The sun was setting by the time Wagner and Becker left the plaza and started back to the hotel. Having a plan, well, a rough idea anyway, Becker felt better about the mission. "How do we get a car?" he asked Wagner, as they strolled along.

"Don't know," Wagner replied. After a pause, he added, "Maybe Lina can help us with that. Let's stop at Fritz's for a drink before dinner."

• • •

It was Friday and Fritz's was jammed with the after-work crowd. When they entered, Wagner and Becker stood in the doorway looking for a table. There were none available. Knowing it was an unwritten rule that officers didn't sit at the bar, they turned to leave. When Lina noticed them, she pushed her way through the throng of partygoers and caught them before they were out the door.

"Lina!" Wagner exclaimed when she approached and took his sleeve. "How nice to see you." Before Lina could reply, he added, "Are you closing the bar tonight?"

Thinking the question was unusual, Lina

wrinkled her brow and replied, "Why, yes. Why do you ask?"

"Just wondering," Wagner said. He then looked at his watch, Lina followed him with her eyes. When he pointed to the number two on the dial, Lina nodded. She realized he was asking for an after-hours meeting behind the bar.

· · ·

Upon securing a meeting with Lina, Wagner and Becker went to their room and freshened up before going to the officer's mess. Before they entered the hotel, Wagner asked, "Do you think my exchange with Klaus this morning will affect us adversely?"

Becker, remembering the anxiety he experienced over the debacle cringed. He just shrugged. *Hopefully, after that scare, Wagner will tone it down.*

When they entered the dining room, most of the other officers were already seated. Wagner and Becker were escorted to the table they occupied before. Captain Schultz and Captain Fischer stood as they approached. "Good evening," Fischer said, and extending his hand, asked, "May I pour you a glass of wine?"

"Good evening to you, as well," Becker immediately replied, not giving Wagner a chance to alienate anyone else. "And yes, we'd like a glass of wine." *Make it the whole bottle.*

"Splendid!" Fischer said as he poured the wine. Wagner and Becker took their seats. Both seemed surprised by the warm reception. *Wonder if Wagner's confrontation with Klaus elevated our status among the other officers,* Becker thought and looked at Wagner. Wagner's expression remained stoic.

After they were seated, Wagner glanced at the head table. Klaus's seat was vacant. Because Becker was seated with his back toward the head-table, Wagner slightly nodded in the direction of the head table. Taking the hint, Becker purposefully dropped his napkin and when he bent to pick it up, he was able to sneak a peek at the head table. Seeing Klaus was absent, fear immediately gripped him. *Wonder what that means?*

• • •

A very observant Captain Fischer, having noticed the exchange between Wagner and Becker, said, "Let me pour another round." As he poured the wine, he said, "I see you've noticed our Captain Klaus is absent."

"Yes," Wagner said. "Is he ill?"

"Not exactly. You see, Klaus, although only a captain, thinks and acts like he's commander in chief. He's had many confrontations with fellow officers. *Der Führer* is radical about his officers being united and doesn't take discourse lightly." Fischer paused, and looking at the head table, took a sip of wine before continuing, "I understand Klaus has been recalled to Berlin and then most likely he will be sent to the front."

Wagner was stunned when he realized he, most likely, was the straw that broke the camel's back. *The front is a death sentence. Will I be considered a hero or a pariah by the other officers?* Conversation during the rest of dinner was sparse. The message was clear. It appeared they each were reflecting on Klaus's destiny.

Wagner's question was soon answered when the others in attendance began to leave the dining room. He was surprised when a major walked up to their table and extended his hand. "Captain Wagner," the major said, "I'm Major Goldstein. Welcome to our facility. Let me know if there's anything we can do for you?"

"Thank you, Major," Wagner said as he shook Goldstein's hand. Much to Wagner's disbelief, more officers stopped by their table, introduced themselves, and shook his hand as they were leaving. Wagner looked at Becker. Becker raised his brow and smiled.

$\bullet\bullet\bullet$

Wagner and Becker went back to their room after dinner to await their meeting with Lina. They did little talking, still exercising caution that their room may be bugged, especially now that Wagner was deemed to be a hero.

. . .

Just before two, Wagner and Becker left the hotel and rounded the corner entering to the alley which led to Fritz's back entrance. The early morning was cold and they huddled close to the building as they waited for Lina outside the back door. Winter was definitely on the way. Overcoats were scarce and they shivered in the cold, dark alleyway. The back door to Fritz's suddenly opened, and Lina stuck her head out and motioned for them to enter.

"I'm sorry for the wait," Lina said apologetically. "A few customers had to be coaxed to leave."

"That's okay," Wagner said, rubbing his hands together to warm them. He glanced around the bar feeling uneasy and exposed. Satisfied they were alone, he said, "It looks like we're going to proceed with our mission in a few days. Can you get us a car?"

Lina furrowed her brow, apparently weighing her options. Remembering Albert Koch and his bevy of resources, she finally blurted, "Yes, yes, I think I can."

"But," Becker interrupted, "can you do it

without putting yourself in danger?"

"I have a loyal friend who deals in odd jobs. I will not be jeopardized."

"Okay, get one as soon as possible." Wagner said in a commanding tone and looked at Becker. Becker nodded.

Lina frowned, "That may be as soon as tomorrow."

Becker said, "Perfect. The sooner, the better. Just let us know."

• • •

The next evening, Lina was again helping serve in the officer's dining room. When she came to Wagner, she leaned forward moving his water glass to make room for his dinner plate, she knocked his napkin onto his lap. When she retrieved the napkin, she slipped a note into its folds. Wagner, now a professional at hiding surprise, didn't even wince. He just continued the conversation he was having with Fischer. Pretending to stifle a cough, Wagner reached into his hip pocket and extracted his handkerchief. After dabbing at his nose, he surreptitiously wadded the note into the handkerchief, and placed it in his hip pocket.

Eager to read the note, it seemed to Wagner that dinner dragged on longer than usual. When at last the diners began to disburse, Wagner rose and said to his dinner companions, "It's been a long day. I think I'll go to bed early, so, if you'll excuse me…"

"Of course," Captain Fischer replied. "I think I'll follow suit."

Becker and Schultz also stood and followed Wagner and Fischer out of the dining hall.

• • •

Back in their room, Wagner unfolded the handkerchief and opened the note. Together, Wagner and Becker read:

> **Later tonight there will be a small**
> **blue car parked in front of your hotel.**
> **The keys will be in the ignition.**

Becker immediately began gathering their belongings, getting ready to leave. It was obvious they wouldn't be able to return to the hotel and he was anxious to get *Operation Juggernaut* behind them. So far, they had been lucky but luck, he remembered, is a fickle mistress. When they returned to the hotel, they changed into the ski pants and sweaters previously provided by Lina. Taking every precaution, they folded their German uniforms into one of the garment bags thinking they might need them if they survived after the explosion. It was now a waiting game.

They could see the curb in front of the hotel

from their second story window and they took turns keeping a steady vigilance watching for the car Lina had described. The hours ticked by slowly as they watched and waited. Becker was at the window when he saw a small, blue car pull up and park in front of their hotel. Excited, and in his haste to alert Wagner, he didn't wait to see who got out of the car.

As soon as Becker gave Wagner the high sign, Wagner was on his feet. Taking one last look around to ensure they had covered their tracks, he motioned to Becker and they picked up their bags and left, taking the back stairs to the alleyway behind the hotel. They slowly crept around the corner and looked up and down the street. It was late and the street was dark and deserted. Satisfied they hadn't been detected, they approached the vehicle. Becker eased open the rear door and placed their belongings on the passenger side floor. In his rush to get going, he didn't notice Lina huddled in the corner of the rear seat on the driver's side. She held her breath and remained very still until they were out of town.

Wagner was driving and Becker navigating. When they came to a fork in the road, Wagner slowed down and asked. "Which way?"

Becker hesitated. "I'm not sure. Go right, I think," he finally said.

Wagner, already in an anxious state, blurted, "You're not sure! Go right you think! That's just great. We can't afford to—"

Both men were startled when a voice came from the back seat, "Take the left fork." They were relieved when they realized it was Lina's voice.

Wagner was the first to react. "Lina! What in the hell are you doing here?" he shouted as he turned and stared at her.

"I'm going with you!" she exclaimed and rushed on before they could object. "I've already earned my keep by preventing you from taking the wrong fork in the road. You can't do this without me. Now take the left fork and let's get going."

They realized they couldn't take Lina back to town, and that she was right, they couldn't do it without her. Accepting the fact that she was going with them, Wagner took the left fork. It was full speed ahead.

• • •

When they approached the entrance to the tunnel, Wagner stopped the vehicle on a curve so that it wouldn't be detected by the guards. After carefully surveilling the area, they determined only one guard was on duty at the entrance of the tunnel. That seemed strange since the tunnel was indispensable in furnishing military supplies, equipment, and personnel to the German army. *Had their presence been detected?* Becker wondered as he swiveled his head in disbelief at the pitiful lack of security.

The guard was drinking from a canteen and appeared to be at ease. He was standing in the open. Without cover, there was no way to sneak up on him. Finally, Lina put her finger to her lips. Still dressed in the waitress dirndl, she stepped out into the open and began to walk toward the guard before Wagner or Becker could stop her. There was nothing they could do without causing a disturbance so they crouched down and watched.

When Lina was in close proximity to the guard, she slowed her walk and began to trace the lines of her hips with her hands in a seductive manner. When the guard noticed her, he looked shocked.

"Where'd you come from?" he demanded and craned his neck trying to look past her while reaching for his service revolver.

"What difference does it make?" Lina cooed. "I'm here now." She smiled sweetly at him.

"So you are," were his last words. Becker had slipped up behind the guard when Lina had his attention. He grabbed the guard around the shoulders and stabbed him in the back with his knife.

Before Becker could turn, a second guard

appeared from out of nowhere and pounced on him. From his position, Wagner saw the second guard coming and raced to Becker's aid. Before the guard could land a second blow on Becker, Wagner had one arm around the guard's neck in a choke hold. Using his other hand, he twisted the guard's head, breaking his neck. The guard went limp and fell.

Lina gasped as the horror unfolded before her eyes. The horror of war was something she could never get used to. Afraid she would scream, Becker placed a hand over her mouth. "Lina," he whispered, "this is war. We have a mission to complete. If we allowed the guards to live, they would've sounded the alarm and none of us would be alive to talk about it. All of this would be for naught. The mission would end in failure."

When Lina realized she had almost compromised the mission, she nodded, and Becker removed his hand from her mouth. "I don't like killing any more than you," he said. "However, when you're fighting a war, often decisions are made in the blink of an eye and it's kill or be killed." It was apparent he felt no sympathy for her when, after a pause, he added, "You're the one who decided to come with us."

Lina nodded again and hung her head. Wagner had been listening to Becker. Although he thought

Becker's words were unduly harsh, he chose not to comment. Instead, he said in a hushed tone, "I've been thinking. The car is small enough to drive through the tunnel. We can load the kegs of gunpowder into the trunk and transport them midway and unload them, saving one keg of gunpowder to use in our getaway. After unloading the explosives, we'll drive the rest of the way through the tunnel trailing a line of gunpowder behind us. When we ignite the trail of gunpowder, we'll be on the Austrian side when the dynamitebomb explodes." After a pause, he asked, "What do you think?"

"Hell, yes, man." Becker said. "That's ingenious."

Chapter Seven
———

Detonation

Wagner retrieved the car and drove it to the shed. Lina changed into her ski pants and a sweater while the men loaded the gunpowder and dynamite into the trunk of the car. When they were ready, all three got into the car and Becker began to drive through the tunnel. They deemed it safe to use the headlights since they were inside the tunnel. When they reached what they thought to be midway, Lina waited in the car while Wagner and Becker distributed the gunpowder which led to the dynamite bomb in the middle of the tunnel. They took the last keg of gunpowder, created an opening in the lid, and turned it on its side. Following the car, Wagner rolled the keg through the tunnel to the Austrian side, creating a trail of gunpowder.

When they cleared the tunnel, Wagner motioned for Becker to move the car a safe distance from the entrance. Not knowing if they had been detected by either side, Wagner didn't take time to check their work. He took a stick match from his breast pocket and struck it on the side of the tunnel. As soon as the flame appeared, he tossed it onto the trail of gunpowder. It ignited with a swoosh and began methodically traveling toward the bomb. Wagner raced to the car, jumped in, and instructed Becker to take off.

A few moments later, they heard the blast of the bomb and felt the tremor. Becker stopped the car and all three looked back. Black smoke was pouring from the entrance of the tunnel and they could hear the thunderous roar of an angry mountain later described by some as a cataclysmic event. Now, instead of going through the Bavarian Alps, the convoys would have to either go around or over the vast expanse of the imposing mountain range. No more shortcut!

The trio of saboteurs watched for a few moments before leaving the scene. "Looks like it worked," Becker said and punched Wagner on the biceps before putting the car in gear.

Wagner dropped his head back against the seat, "Thank, God," he whispered.

Lina just sat in stunned silence. She was still in deep prayer.

• • •

A few moments after the explosion, the night was shattered with the blare of air raid sirens. "We've got to get outta here!" Becker barked. "They'll soon have the roads closed."

"Let's do it," Wagner said. Looking back at Lina, he asked, "Any idea where we are?"

Lina leaned forward and staring out of the windshield said, "I know exactly where we are. Stay on this road and go straight through the barracks. There's a dirt country road on the other side. I know where it goes."

Becker hesitated. "You sure?" he asked.

"Yes, I'm sure. We don't have time to argue," Lina said, irritation evident in her voice. "Now, go!"

Becker jammed on the gas and followed Lina's instructions. As they progressed through the barracks, they encountered a number of vehicles coming from the opposite direction moving toward the tunnel. Motivated by fear, Becker drove like a bat outta hell. As soon as they cleared the military base, they found themselves on a dirt road, just as Lina said.

"Where does this road go?" Wagner asked.

"Innsbruck," Lina responded. "That's where I grew up. Hopefully, our house is still standing."

Becker looked at her in amazement. "How far?" he asked, as he checked the gas gauge.

"Less than fifty miles."

• • •

Captain Bauer was violently awakened by the explosion. Jumping from his bed, he pulled on his uniform pants and raced in the direction of the chaos. He encountered two guards as he left the building.

"What was that?" he shouted.

"The tunnel has been sabotaged," one of the guards panted, as he ran alongside the major. Bauer stopped in his tracks apparently stunned when he was told the tunnel had been destroyed. "How in the hell did that happen! Didn't we have guards on duty?" he demanded.

"Yes, sir. But we don't know where they are."

"What do you mean, you don't know where they are?"

"We haven't been able to locate them yet."

"Oh, mein Gott, you mean someone was able to breach our security…"

"Yes, sir.

"How severe is the damage?" Bauer asked, wiping sweat from his brow with his hand.

"We haven't had time to assess the damage—" the guard began.

"That's not good enough!" Bauer roared, spewing spittle in his anger. Both guards cowered. They knew full well someone would have to pay a heavy price. It was certain Bauer wasn't going to take the blame. All Bauer had to do was find a scapegoat if the culprits were not caught.

Approaching the entrance to the tunnel, Bauer noticed Engineer Herman Steiner assessing the devastation. It was apparent he couldn't possibly see anything as black smoke continued to pour from the tunnel.

"Herr Steiner!" Bauer shouted. When Steiner didn't respond, Bauer shouted louder, "Herr Steiner!" When Steiner finally turned, the look on his face was pure terror.

"Captain Bauer," he said and headed in the major's direction.

"What happened here!" Bauer demanded. His expression bespoke of irritability and no tolerance to a flimsy excuse.

"It's too soon to make a prediction, but my guess is sabotage," Steiner replied. It was obvious he was trying to divert culpability away from himself and his crew.

Just then a guard rushed up. "Captain Bauer," he blurted.

"Yes! What is it!"

"We found the guards. They're both dead. One stabbed and the other had his neck broken."

Bauer sagged and rubbed the back of his neck. "Then it was sabotage."

The guard took a step back, apparently hoping to avoid a tongue lashing by the major.

"Herr Steiner," Bauer said, "how long before you can make a determination as to the cause of the explosion?"

Looking toward the tunnel, Steiner said, "Not for a while. We'll have to wait for the smoke to clear before we can do an examination. And then it may not be safe to enter the tunnel. The initial explosion could cause a major collapse of the entire tunnel." Steiner looked around apparently seeking an avenue to avoid Bauer's wrath. When his eyes fell on the shack where they stored the explosives, he suddenly remembered the two inspectors and their unusual interest in the ammunition stash.

"Sir," Steiner said.

"Yes, what is it?" Bauer responded.

"Remember when the two captains showed up to inspect the facility?"

Obviously irritated, Bauer said, "Yes, what about it?"

"Well, they seemed particularly interested in the shack where the explosives were stored."

With renewed interest, Bauer turned and looked at the shack. "Would you know if any of your inventory was missing?"

"Yes!" Steiner said. "We can check with the inventory report I have posted at the entrance of the shack.

"Go examine your supplies and report back to me."

"Yes, sir," Steiner said, relieved to have redirected Bauer's outrage.

"We must inform headquarters of the breach immediately." He turned toward the radio shack. Then turning back to Steiner, he asked, "Do you remember the names of the captains?"

"Captain Wagner and Captain Becker!" Steiner spat out the names. "Two very rude officers."

Recalling how Wagner and Becker barged into his office without knocking, Bauer nodded. Smiling, he made a mental note to implicate Captains Wagner and Becker as being involved in the sabotage when he sent his transmission to headquarters. *Revenge is sweetest when served cold.*

• • •

Feeling more secure because of the havoc created by the explosion, no one paid attention to the obscure beat-up blue car going the opposite direction toward Innsbruck. Less than an hour into their escape, leaning forward with her hands on the back of the front seat, Lina directed Becker to take a side road.

"This lane leads to my home," she said, and her voice cracked with emotion.

Wagner turned in his seat and took one of her

hands. "Lina, we couldn't have done it without you. You're one of the bravest people I know."

• • •

Moments later, Becker stopped in front of a small white cottage. Lina sat transfixed staring at the house. Wagner and Becker stepped out of the car. Each took a different direction and circled the house meeting back at the car.

"Looks safe," Wagner said. He opened the rear door and beckoned Lina out of the car. Lina's hand shook as she took his. She trembled and tears streamed down her face. She was obviously emotional at being home after all these years and all that had happened, especially after just recently finding out about the deaths of her parents.

Becker drove the car to the back of the cottage to hide it from prying eyes. He met Wagner and Lina at the front door. When they entered the cottage, they walked through a curtain of cobwebs.

"Damn!" Becker blurted, as he swiped at the webs from his face. "I hate those things!"

Ignoring Becker's outburst, and still concerned for their safety. Hoping to distract Lina from her melancholy, Wagner asked, "How close are your neighbors?"

Lina, looking thoughtful for the moment, finally said, "At least a quarter of a mile away. My father's property encompasses about a quarter of a mile in each direction." Lina went to the cupboard and took out several candles. "I think it would be safe to have some light," she said as she put three candles into metal holders and lit them with a wooden match she took from the cupboard. She handed Wagner and Becker each a candle.

Pointing to an open doorway, she said, "That's my parents' room. Feel free to use it. My room is behind the kitchen. I think we're safe, at least for the time being. Anyway, there's nothing we can do here in the dark. I'll see you tomorrow morning."

"Thank you, Lina," Wagner said.

Lina nodded and went toward her room. The men turned toward their room. Even though they were pumped emotionally, they were exhausted physically. Without bothering to turn the dusty coverlet back, they took off their shoes and flopped down on the bed. In the candle light, they discussed the possibility of escape.

"What do you think our chances are?" Becker asked.

"You want an honest opinion?"

"Hell, yes!" Becker answered. "This is not the time for diplomacy! Three lives are hanging in the balance—yours and mine included."

"Okay, since you insist, but you're not gonna

like my answer. In my opinion, our chances are zero to none," Wagner replied as he stifled a yawn.

Becker commented "That good, huh?"

Wagner blew out his candle. "I'm beat, Buddy. We completed *Operation Juggernaut* in accordance with our instructions, and I quote, merciless, destructive, and unstoppable. General Rochester will be proud of us. We'll probably receive a posthumous medal."

"Hell, I'm proud of us!" Becker snorted. "And what's this posthumous bull? I intend to survive so I can tell my grandchildren the Tale of the Juggernaut." A moment later, he said, "I'd like to have been a mouse at German headquarters when they were told of the devastation."

"Yeah. We miss all the fun. 'Night," mumbled a groggy Wagner.

"'Night," Becker said, "and good work." Soon both men were snoring. It had been a day from hell.

• • •

The next morning, Wagner and Becker were awakened by clattering coming from the kitchen, and the aroma of something cooking permeated the house.

"Where are we?" groaned Becker.

Swinging his legs over the side of the bed, Wagner said, "Come on, hit the deck. Sounds like our hostess is cooking something."

"I just hope it isn't squirrel."

"Hold your nose and you won't taste it," Wagner teased.

"Does that really work?" Becker asked.

Wagner didn't answer. He was already out of the room. After taking turns visiting the outhouse, Wagner and Becker entered the kitchen. Much to their surprise, they saw the countertop laden with jars of canned fruit and vegetables.

Lina turned. "Good morning," she chirped.

"Yes, yes, it is," Wagner replied. "What's all of this?" he asked pointing to the jars.

"We have my mother to thank for this. She canned everything she could get her hands on and stored the jars in the root cellar behind the house—even oats and wheat." Looking heavenward, Lina said, "Thank you, Mother."

"Amen," both men said in unison.

Wiping her hands on her apron, Lina nodded toward the wood cook stove. "I've prepared breakfast. There's a pump out back you can use to wash," she said and handed them each a towel as she pointed to the backdoor with a wooden spoon.

• • •

When the trio was gathered around the table, Lina made the sign of the cross. Wagner and

Becker bowed their heads in silent thanksgiving as Lina recited an age-old German prayer. "Come, Lord Jesus, be our guest, and let Thy gifts to us be blessed."

"Amen," Wagner and Becker said in unison.

As they ate hot oatmeal and sliced peaches, Becker said, "This is the best breakfast I've ever had. Thank you, Lina, thank you."

Lina blushed. "You're welcome, but my mother…" Lina stopped midsentence. Dissolving in tears, she covered her face with her hands.

Sensing something more was going on than just being home amidst the memories of her parents, Wagner reached across the table and took Lina's hand. "What is it, Lina?"

Gently pulling her hand free, Lina took her napkin and dabbed at her eyes. She then folded her hands in her lap, and through bouts of tears, she told them about how she'd been deceived into spying for the Nazis in order to save her parents. She told them that, after Karl disclosed to her that her parents had been shot on their way to Dachau, she vowed to get even. That's when she became a double agent.

After hearing her story, Wagner thought, Now it all makes sense. Slapping his palm on the tabletop, Wagner addressed both Lina and Becker, "By damn! This story doesn't end here! We will escape,

I promise you—and I never, never break a promise!"

The room became eerily silent for a few moments. Finally, Becker asked, "Does that mean you have a plan?"

Wagner hesitated before replying, "Not yet, but I will."

As Becker helped Lina with the dishes, Wagner wandered outside and sat down on the wooden porch railing. When Becker and Lina joined him, pointing to the mountain Wagner asked, "Is there a way we can get across the mountain on foot?"

"Possible but not practical. It would take at least three weeks to hike across. Plus, we don't have provisions or appropriate equipment or clothing. It would be suicide." Then looking at Wagner, Lina said, "We're about a hundred and eighty miles from the Swiss border. If we could get—"

"What! Only one eighty! Now, that's more like it!" Wagner exclaimed. After a pause, he asked, "Is there a place to get fuel for the car between here and the border?"

"I don't know," Lina said. "I've never traveled that route. The tank was full when Karl delivered it. We've gone less than twenty-five miles so there should be enough left to at least get us three-quarters of the way to the border, maybe farther. And if we run out, we could hike the remaining distance.

Wagner nodded. "I noticed some winter clothing in your parents' room, Lina. Would you be opposed to us using—"

"Not at all. Dad had several pairs of boots and winter outerwear which I think will fit the two of you. I'll use Mother's. I was just a girl when we were forced to leave here. I had much smaller feet then." After a pause she added, "We also have some rucksacks."

"Splendid!" Wagner exclaimed. "We'll put the uniforms in the rucksacks. Who knows, they may come in handy when—or if— we get back to civilization."

"You mean *when* we get back to civilization. Remember, nothing worth doing ever came easy," said Becker.

"When did you become so poetic and optimistic?" Wagner teased.

"Always. That's just a side of me you've never seen." Stepping up to the railing, Becker looked at the sky. "The clouds are gathering over the mountain," he said. "We don't have any time to lose. It looks like a storm is brewing."

"I noticed that earlier. We'll use the rest of the day to get organized and leave first thing tomorrow morning," Wagner said. Then turning to Lina, added, "Where are the rucksacks?"

"There's a small room off the kitchen, Lina replied. "Dad used that closet to store off-season supplies."

• • •

It was close to three by the time the men gathered miscellaneous items of clothing needed for the trip. They folded the German uniforms and their other clothing into the rucksacks and took them to the car.

In the meantime, Lina raided her mother's closet. When she slipped on her mother's wool coat with the fake fur collar, she detected a hint of the cologne her mother always wore. Feeling warm and cozy, Lina gathered the coat around her. It was the same feeling she had when, as a child, her mother snuggled her in her arms. Lina hugged the coat close to her. "Thank you, Mother," she whispered as she swiped tears from her cheeks.

• • •

When the men finished assembling their gear for the trip, they entered the kitchen. Lina was preoccupied with preparing a meal. She had already set the table and was putting the finishing touches on a pot of soup.

"Is that what I think it is?" Wagner asked as he peered over her shoulder into the steaming pot.

"What do you think it is?" Lina asked good-naturedly.

"Chicken noodle soup?"

"You get the prize. It is chicken noodle soup." "But where'd you get the chicken?" Wagner asked looking around the kitchen apparently expecting to see blood, guts and feathers strewn about.

"Mother made large batches of our favorites when she cooked so she would have enough to can. They, my parents, went through some lean times. They never wasted anything, and she, very wisely, planned ahead." Lina picked up a wooden ladle and said, "Are you ready to try her soup?"

"Are you kidding?" Becker snorted and headed for the table. He didn't need to be coaxed. The aroma was enticement enough.

When they were assembled at the table, they were filled with the excited expectation that they would escape the Nazis. Faith and hope spurred them on, and Wagner and Becker each took one of Lina's hands. Together the three of them said the prayer Lina had said at breakfast.

"Come, Lord Jesus, be our guest, and let Thy gifts to us be blessed."

As he crossed himself, Becker thought, *And Lord, bless our journey, not just the food.*

"This is the best chicken soup I've ever had,"

said Becker when he stopped eating long enough to take a breath.

"That's what you said about breakfast," Wagner pointed out.

Becker just smiled and continued eating.

"Thank you," Lina said. "However, Mother gets the credit, I just warmed it up."

The men helped Lina with the after-dinner cleanup. When the job was completed, Becker yawned and said, "I think I'll turn in early since we'll be leaving before sunup."

"Me, too," Wagner said. "No telling how much sleep we'll get during our journey."

• • •

Upon rising at dawn the next day, and after another hearty breakfast of oatmeal and peaches, the men put the sacks into the car. When Lina returned the unopened jars of canned goods to the cellar, she gathered several jars of dried apples, berries, and jerky and carried them to the kitchen. She emptied the contents of the jars into paper bags, folded the openings over several times to secure the seal, and took the bags out to the car.

"What's this?" Wagner asked as he accepted the bags.

"Jerky, dried apples, and berries—for the trip," Lina answered.

Carefully placing the bags in the backseat, Wagner said, "Your mother was quite a woman. She thought of everything."

"Yes, she did," Lina replied. "Wonder if she knows…"

Looking heavenward, Wagner said reassuringly, "I'm sure she does, Lina, I'm sure she does."

Chapter Eight

Retaliation

Upon learning that their crucial tunnel through the Alps had been destroyed and that two Nazi officers were allegedly involved, the Nazis immediately closed all roads within a hundred-mile radius. Their hope was to capture the perpetrators before they could make their getaway. The Riech was unforgiving, especially toward their own. Failure was not a viable alternative.

Commander Hoffmann, the officer in charge of Nazi headquarters in Ravensnest, paced the floor before his subordinates who were lined up in his office.

"They must have had help to have pulled this off!" he shouted. "Interrogate all the locals! I want whoever was involved to pay for this treason!" Pointing to the door, he roared, "Schnell! Schnell!"

"Yes, sir," the rank and file shouted in unison. They nearly ran over each other getting out of Hoffmann's office.

• • •

Ravensnest was a small, closeknit community. Word of the tunnel disaster and possible sabotage spread like wildfire throughout the area. Knowing the German propensity for cruelty and intolerance, the locals shuddered to think of the retaliation that would be leveled on the community if one of their peers was deemed to be involved.

While waiting for the interrogations to begin, people went about their everyday activities. Captain Burger, and the quickly assembled interrogators, had the locals brought to a sterile office at police headquarters for questioning. The idea was to intimidate them by removing them from their comfort zone, and hopefully cause them to reveal anything they knew about the tunnel disaster.

When Fritz noticed Lina hadn't reported for work and hadn't called in sick, he assembled his employees for a meeting. "Where's Lina?" he asked when they were all gathered in the bar area. He waited for a few moments, and when no one offered an explanation, he asked, "Does anyone know who she was friendly with?" Still, no one volunteered an answer.

Fritz furrowed his brow. "With Lina mysteriously disappearing, and so soon after Deiter dying in the bar, it's beginning to look like she may be involved."

When Fritz was taken to police headquarters for questioning, Burger showed him the photos of Wagner and Becker taken from their identification badges. "Do you recognize these two men?" Burger asked.

Upon examining the photos, Fritz remembered Lina having been unusually friendly with the two captains. *What has Lina gotten herself into?* Not wanting to cause Lina, and most likely himself as her employer, trouble with the Germans, Fritz responded, "Yes, they were regulars at the bar."

"I see. Do you know where they're staying?"

"I believe at the hotel next to the bar. That's where most of the military personnel are quartered," Fritz answered.

"Do you know if they were friendly with any of the local population and Lina in particular?"

"No, sir." Fritz answered.

Apparently disappointed at not having gained any worthwhile information, Burger removed his glasses and said, "That'll be all…for now. You may go."

Burger's words *for now* stuck in Fritz's mind. Did that mean he would he be interrogated again? He groaned thinking what his fate would be if it were determined that he was withholding critical information. He was caught between a rock and a hard spot. Yet, Lina's involvement was speculative at best.

• • •

As soon as Fritz left, Burger summoned two military police and ordered them to conduct a search of Wagner's and Becker's room at the hotel. It was not a surprise when, after a thorough search, it was reported back to him that the room was completely empty. There was no sign of anyone having stayed there.

• • •

The three saboteurs were within a few miles of the Swiss border before they ran out of fuel. They ditched their car in a grove of trees and walked to the border. When they approached the land entry station at the Austrian-Switzerland border they were stopped by a border patrol guard. He apparently saw them coming and lowered the gate preventing them from crossing the line into Switzerland.

"Halt!" the guard ordered as he sized up the three travelers. "Why do you seek entrance into Switzerland?"

Wagner took the lead. "We're sightseers traveling the country."

The guard looked perplexed. "During a war?"

"Yes," Wagner replied without hesitation,

hoping he wouldn't have to come up with any further explanation.

Then, apparently looking for the means of how these three just happened to appear out of nowhere, the guard looked past the vagabonds, and asked, "How long do you intend to stay?"

"We're not sure. We're on sabbatical from the university. We've been traveling and doing some research for our thesis."

The guard scratched his head and asked, "How'd you get here?"

"Why does that matter?" Wagner replied.

The guard looked disgruntled.

Sensing Wagner was nearing the end of his very short rope, Becker blurted, "We're on our way to Liechtenstein. Is there any public transportation available?"

"Ja! This station is the bus stop. The bus travels from here to Liechtenstein with a few stops in between. It's a three-hour trip. Many farmers use the bus to go into the city to conduct business. The bus makes the turn at this point." Checking his watch, the guard said, "You're in luck. Here comes the bus now, right on time."

Not sure what to do with the three vagabonds, the guard opted not to make an issue out of the crossing.

. . .

When the bus stopped at the port of entry, its passengers alighted. While talking to the guard, Wagner had noticed some cars parked behind the guard house. The debussing passengers headed toward the parked vehicles. A few women were carrying packages with logos advertising shops.

As soon as all the passengers had exited, the driver motioned to Wagner, Becker, and Lina to come aboard. Wagner was the last to board. After paying the fare for the three of them, he asked the driver, "Is there an American Embassy in Liechtenstein?"

"Yes, sir. In fact, it's a regular stop on my route. I'll let you know when we get there," the driver said, as he closed the door and put the bus in gear. When the bus lurched forward, Wagner staggered and had to steady himself by holding onto a pole next to the driver's seat.

"Thank you," Wagner said. When he turned toward the rear of the bus, he noticed Becker was stretched out full length on the row of back seats. Lina was curled up on a seat midway. It appeared they were both asleep. Wagner opted to take the seat behind the driver. They were the only passengers on the bus and the driver was friendly, not hostile like the guard at the port entry. Feeling somewhat secure, he, too, soon fell asleep.

It felt like they had just gotten underway when the driver turned and said to Wagner, "We're here. That's the embassy straight ahead."

Struggling to wake up, Wagner rubbed sleep from his eyes. He craned his neck in order to see out of the windshield. The building in front of him was a large, red brick structure. The first thing he noticed was an American flag suspended from a flagpole on the front lawn of the embassy, gently waving in the breeze. Wagner could no longer control his emotions and fought the tears as he gazed at it.

"Not many people come to the embassy," the driver said, as he maneuvered the bus toward the curb. Slowing the bus, he said, "Although there's a circular drive, I usually just drop passengers off on the street in front of the embassy." Looking back at Wagner, he added, "I'll take you and your friends to the front entrance."

Still groggy and seeped in emotion, Wagner whispered, "Thank you."

• • •

Awakened by the conversation between Wagner and the bus driver, Becker and Lina moved to the front of the bus. When Becker saw the stars and stripes in front of the embassy, he punched

Wagner on the biceps. Wagner just grinned and winked at Becker.

"Not quite, but this is a good start," Wagner responded. "We still have a long way to go, but things are looking up."

When the bus driver stopped the bus and opened the door, he looked back at the trio who were anxiously waiting in the aisle. He said, "Good luck, to wherever your quest takes you, and may God go with you."

Wagner clasped the driver's hand and shook it vigorously. He then stepped from the bus. Becker shouldered their rucksacks, and he and Lina followed, both thanking the driver as they left. In the time it took Becker and Lina to get off the bus, Wagner was already on the embassy portico ringing the bell. Becker and Lina rushed to join him. Although they were in a neutral country, Becker, still feeling exposed, kept looking over his shoulder. *So far, so good!*

• • •

"Good afternoon," a middle-aged nondescript woman dressed in a maid's uniform said when she opened the door.

"And to you, too," Wagner replied with a smile. "Thank you, sir. How can we be of service?" the maid asked as she sized up the three.

"We're Americans seeking asylum from the Nazis," Becker exclaimed, cutting Wagner off before he could say too much.

Wagner didn't notice, or chose to ignore Becker's interruption.

Looking frenzied by having Americans show up on the doorstep, the maid gasped and stepped back. After a moment, she regained her composure and opened the door wider. "Please come in… I'll let Ambassador Woodard know you're here."

After the maid left, Becker said to Wagner, "Sounds like they're expecting us."

"Not likely. She appeared to be shocked when you announced who we were. Besides, when we left Ravensnest, we didn't even know where we were headed."

In a matter of a few moments, a trim, clean-shaven, middle-aged man entered the foyer. "Welcome to the American Embassy," he said as he walked toward them with his hand extended. My name is Torance Woodard, current American Ambassador here in Switzerland."

Wagner shook the ambassador's hand and introduced the three of them.

"Happy to meet you," Ambassador Woodard said. "Come into my office. I'll have Hilda bring coffee. In the interim, you can tell me about your plight."

• • •

Over coffee and pastries, Wagner and Becker took turns explaining their circumstances. As soon as they told the ambassador about blowing up the tunnel, he exclaimed, "Oh! So, you're the culprits!" Following a hearty laugh, the ambassador wiped tears from his eyes, slammed his palm on his desktop, and chortled, "Good work! That little escapade threw a wrench into the Nazi war machine." After a brief pause, his reaction subsided a bit and he whispered, "I hear you made Hitler's most-wanted list. He just doesn't know your identities."

Taken aback by suddenly realizing the magnitude of their daring act, Wagner, Becker, and Lina just sat and stared at the ambassador.

After a moment, the ambassador said, "You have the Nazis running in circles. They immediately blocked all the roads. How'd you get here?"

Still feeling uneasy, and not wanting to reveal how they escaped, Becker immediately intervened before Wagner could say anything, "Divine intervention, Ambassador, divine intervention."

Ambassador Woodard nodded. "I should say so," he said, apparently understanding their reluctance to go into detail. After a pause, he added, "We must get you back to the United States as soon as possible. We have an excellent underground network here in Liechtenstein. I'll contact the locals right away and get the extraction process started."

"Thank you," Wagner said. "But…"

The ambassador raised his brow. "Yes?"

Wagner continued, "But, I'm puzzled, sir. How'd you find out about the sabotage so quickly?"

"Although Switzerland is a neutral country, America is not. The embassy is considered to be on American soil. However, like I said, we have an excellent underground." Clearing his throat, the ambassador continued, "The information I received only mentioned two males impersonating German officers were being sought by the Germans." He nodded toward Lina, "How does your companion fit in?"

Wagner looked at Lina and smiled. "We could not have pulled it off without Lina's help."

Apparently recognizing he had hit a brick wall; the ambassador dropped the subject. "Of course. I'll have Hilda show you to your rooms. Dinner is at seven."

• • •

Hilda had been in her room listening to the ambassador's conversation by way of a device provided to her by the Nazis. The transmitter had been taped to the underside of the middle drawer in the ambassador's desk. As Hilda listened, a thrill of excitement went through her when she heard that the newcomers were responsible for the tunnel disaster. She was so engrossed in her spying, she actually jumped when the buzzer summoning her sounded. She immediately hid her listening device and went to the ambassador's office.

"Yes, sir," she said when she entered.

"Ah, there you are. Hilda, please show our guests to rooms and provide them with whatever they need. They will be staying for a few days."

"Yes, sir," Hilda responded. She was relieved to hear the saboteurs would be staying at the embassy for at least two days, maybe even more. That would give her time to contact her intermediary and arrange for their arrest. She smiled thinking of how she would be honored for having helped capture the saboteurs. W*hy, der Führer may even award me a medal.*

Extraction

Hilda led Wagner, Becker, and Lina up a wide, red-carpeted, circular staircase to the second floor. The embassy was designed to accommodate asylum seekers, and the second floor consisted of a series of bedrooms situated on both sides of a lengthy, wide corridor. A long narrow, glass-topped table stood against one wall. It was flanked by two straight-backed wooden chairs with seats upholstered in intricate tapestry. A large bouquet of fresh flowers, featuring a variety of daisies, edelweiss, and lilies, was positioned in the center of the table under an ornate gold-framed mirror. Lina raised her brow in bewilderment. *Wonder if fresh flowers are the order of the day every day?*

Hilda stopped about half way down the corridor. Pointing to three doors, she said, "These three rooms are available. You may each take your pick. I'll be back in a few minutes with fresh towels. Dinner is always at seven."

"Thank you, Hilda," Lina said. She chose the door in the middle, opened it, and went in. Becker set her rucksack inside the doorway.

He handed Wagner his rucksack, and then he proceeded to the third door and went in.

"Guess that leaves me with the first room," Wagner said loud enough for Becker to hear.

Becker stuck his head out, "Quit complaining," he said, but before he could close the door, Wagner motioned to him. "What's up," Becker whispered as he joined Wagner in front of Wagner's door.

"Our Nazi uniforms," Wagner said. "Apparently, Hilda has access to all the rooms, all the time. Although I have no reason to suspect anything, I've learned to opt on the side of caution."

"I see what you mean." After a pause, Becker asked, "Any solution come to mind?"

"Not unless we want to sandwich them between the mattress and springs. Even then, they may be discovered when the bedding is changed."

After a few moments, Becker said, "I have an idea, how 'bout we put them on hangers and hang our ski sweaters over the top of 'em? We won't be wearing the sweaters inside the embassy."

"Good idea! Even though we don't have any other options, that's still a good idea!" Wagner whispered and nudged Becker with his elbow.

Becker blushed. He wasn't used to being praised, especially by Wagner. "Come on, let's get cleaned up for dinner. I'm starved."

• • •

Alexander "Alex" Larsson, retired U.S. Navy, relocated to Liechtenstein, his ancestral home, after retirement. His story is much like many others, that is, parents migrating to America for a better life. He was born in America but fell in love with Switzerland through the stories his parents shared with him. When he was twelve years old, the family took a vacation trip to Liechtenstein. He was so smitten with the Swiss, he vowed that someday he would return.

Alex joined the Navy when he was eighteen and served his country for 20 years. His unit was part of the American Expeditionary Forces sent to Europe in 1917 during the first world war. The AEF helped turn the war around in favor of Britain and France leading to an Allied victory over Germany and Austria in 1918.

Alex was career-minded, and because of his being deployed most of the time, he never married. He retired at age fifty-nine and moved to Liechtenstein where, through mutual friends, he became acquainted with Ambassador Torance Woodard. Alex had been retired for five years when the U.S. entered World War II. Too old to reenlist, Alex devised a plan on how to best serve the Allies. He recruited several of his fellow retirees, and together they created an effective underground operation in Switzerland.

· · ·

As soon as Hilda showed Wagner, Becker, and Lina to their rooms, Ambassador Woodard began the extraction process. He placed a phone call to Alex Larsson.

"Alex, Woodard here. You're not going to believe what just dropped into our laps."

"Hmm, I've been around the horn a couple of times, try me?" Alex replied.

Alex remained silent listening. At the end of Woodard's astounding disclosure, Alex whistled. "That's some hot potato. What's the current status?"

"We've granted them asylum. Under the circumstances, I'm thinking we'd be wise to get them out of Europe as quickly as possible. I think after the ammunition depot destruction they're at the top of the Nazi's hit list."

"Roger that. Do you have a plan?"

"Yes…you!"

Alex laughed. "That's not much of a plan. I'll get my team together and we'll figure it out. You can let them know you have something in the works."

"Thanks. You always come through for us. With this hot potato extra caution is warranted."

"Agreed. I'll be in touch," Alex promised. Alex

knew there was a sense of urgency to the assignment and that deception was the name of the game. He was also aware of the risks involved. Only he knew if he was up to the task.

• • •

Because of years of listening via her covert device supplied her by the Nazis, Hilda already knew about the underground. However, now it was imperative she find out about the plan to move the Americans so she could pass the information on to the Nazis. During her tenure, whenever the ambassador's office door was closed, she would rush to her room so she could listen in on the conversations. She even shirked some of her duties, feigning headaches in order to listen in to what was transpiring in the ambassador's office.

• • •

Wagner had been napping when a knock on his door awakened him. He immediately jumped up and jerked the door open. Becker and Lina were standing in the corridor.

"We're ready to go to dinner. You want to join us?" Becker asked.

"What time is it?" Wagner asked, as he stifled a yawn.

Becker pulled his shirt sleeve up and looked at his watch. "Six-fifty, exactly."

"Hold on, let me splash some water on my face, and I'll be right with you."

Five minutes later, the trio headed downstairs.

Noticing Lina's attire for the first time, Wagner said, "You look great."

"Thank you," Lina replied. "Hilda brought me a few things. She said this dress would be appropriate for dinner."

"Nice choice," Becker said and smiled.

• • •

When the trio reached the foyer, Ambassador Woodard came out of his office and greeted them. "Right on time," he said, and gestured toward the dining room. When they entered, the ambassador took Lina's elbow and escorted her to the seat to the right of the head table position and pulled out the chair for her. After Lina was seated, he then stood and waited for Wagner and Becker. As soon as everyone was seated, the ambassador looked at Lina and said, "I would be honored if you would say grace."

Surprised, Lina jerked her head up and smiled at the ambassador. "Yes, and it would be *my* honor to say grace. We owe Him so much." Everyone bowed their head as Lina prayed her family prayer, "Come, Lord Jesus, be our guest, and let Thy gifts to us be blessed."

"Thank you, dear. I remember that prayer from my childhood. My mother…" the ambassador's voice cracked and he stopped midsentence. Having just recently gone through the same kind of grief at losing her mother, Lina reached over and grasped his hand. Words were not necessary. After a moment, the ambassador recovered somewhat and rang the small bell positioned next to his napkin, signaling for dinner to be served.

As they waited, the ambassador said, "The American Embassy here in Liechtenstein is lucky enough to have Hans, the best chef in all of Switzerland—or all of Europe for that matter."

Just then, the door between the dining room and kitchen swung open and a waiter appeared carrying a tray laden with scrumptious-smelling food. He placed a dinner plate before each of the guests. The bill of fare was a dish consisting of potatoes, sausage, and leeks smothered in a cream sauce. Each diner was given a side dish of fondue with bite-sized cubes of bread. After distributing the dinner plates, the waiter opened a bottle of wine and filled each glass. As soon as he retreated, the ambassador spread his napkin on his lap indicating for his guests to begin eating.

After taking a few bites, Becker said, "Mr. Ambassador, I must agree with you. Your chef is outstanding."

The ambassador just smiled.

• • •

The crowning glory was a rich dark chocolate dessert served with piping hot coffee. When the waiter placed the dessert before Lina, she sighed. "I shouldn't…but, what the heck?" Throwing caution to the wind, she took her spoon and dived into the decadent ecstasy of the creamy sweet chocolate. From the look on her face, it was apparent she was in heaven.

After dinner, the diners assembled in the ambassador's office. Hilda, having finished her kitchen duties, rushed to her room and engaged the listening device.

"Please, have a seat," the ambassador said. "Would you join me in an after-dinner cigar?" he asked as he pulled the middle desk drawer open to retrieve the cigar box. In his haste, he pulled the drawer out too far and it slipped onto his lap. Embarrassed, he fumbled around, and as he tried to reinsert the drawer, he inadvertently turned it upside down. The contents of the drawer spilled onto the carpet. A puzzled expression crossed the ambassador's face as he stared at the underside of the drawer. "What's this?" he muttered.

Wagner, seated close to the ambassador,

instantly recognized the foreign object as a radio transmitter. He immediately put his finger to his lips. Taking a notepad and pencil from the ambassador's desktop, he wrote:

> ***Your office is bugged. Don't reveal anything, just act normal.***

The ambassador's face flushed. He mouthed the words, "Bugged? Who?"

Wagner shrugged. Then, pointing to the box of cigars lying on the carpet, he asked, "Are those authentic Cuban cigars?"

Looking perplexed for a moment, the ambassador finally got the clue and answered, "Why, yes! Yes, they are. I have a friend who lives in Cuba. He sends me a box every year for Christmas. Would you like one?"

Taking the drawer from the ambassador, Wagner inspected the transmitter as he said, "I would. It's been years since I've had a good cigar." Making sure he didn't disturb the transmitter, Wagner inserted the drawer back into the desk, and with Lina's help, gathered up the objects strewn about on the carpet. Not wanting to create noise by putting objects back into the desk drawer, they carefully placed them on the desktop.

Apparently, still in a state of shock, the

ambassador robotically offered a cigar to Becker. "No, thank you," Becker replied crisply. "Never picked up the habit."

Having recovered from the shock of finding out his office was bugged, the ambassador replied to Becker, "You're a rare breed. Wish I hadn't." He then turned his head and looking out the French doors that led to the garden, said, "Since it's still early, and such a lovely evening, let's take a walk through the garden."

Realizing it would have been almost impossible to bug the garden, a walk would be an opportunity to communicate openly, so they all readily agreed. A cement walkway wound through the garden. Spruce trees were strategically placed between the flower beds and the maple trees had begun to turn fall colors. Avoiding the cigar smoke, Becker and Lina walked ahead of Wagner and the ambassador, however, close enough to hear the conversation.

When they were far enough from the embassy, the ambassador said, "I'm shocked! I apparently have a traitor in my midst."

"Yes. It appears that way. How many employees do you have on site?" Wagner asked.

"Let's see," the ambassador replied and began to identify them. Hilda, Hans, the chef, one kitchen helper, the gardener, and a maintenance man." The ambassador shook his head. "They've all been with me for years. I'm at a loss as to who the traitor could be."

"The Nazis have a way of *influencing* people to spy for them. We'll set a trap and catch the rat," Wagner said.

After a few moments, the ambassador said, "I've been in touch with the underground. They're working on a plan to extract the three of you."

"That's good news," Wagner said. "When your people show up, let's meet with them in the garden. After we're informed of the actual plan, we'll meet in your office and discuss a formidable plan to throw off the opposition. And in the process, maybe we'll get lucky enough to flush out the spy."

"Great idea. In the meantime, we must be careful…" the ambassador said. It was obvious he was still emotional. "Do you think my entire staff is—"

"I doubt it. That would be too risky. Time will tell so let's not rush to judgment," Wagner said. *My money's on that witch, Hilda.*

• • •

The next day, the ambassador received a call from Alex. "If you still have some of that excellent bourbon, I'll drop by this evening and have a drink with you."

"Hell, yes!" the ambassador said. "What time?"

"Eight?" Alex replied.

"Dinner is at seven. I have some guests. Can you join us?"

"Hmm, sounds tempting but I have other plans. See you around eight."

After dinner, the ambassador again suggested they take a walk in the garden. He instructed Hilda to bring Alex out when he arrived.

"Yes, sir," unblinking, Hilda replied. It was apparent she was disappointed the meeting would not take place in the ambassador's office.

• • •

Wagner, Becker, and Lina once again strolled through the garden with the ambassador. When they were far enough from the embassy, the ambassador informed them that they would be meeting with a member of the underground to discuss the extraction plan. Referring to Wagner's suggestion, he also told them of the plan to meet in his office afterward and discuss a pseudo plan—one designed for the traitor to pass along to the Nazis.

Before anyone could respond, the ambassador looked up. "Here comes Alex now!" he said and moved forward to meet him. The two men clasped hands and exchanged greetings. It was obvious they were longtime friends.

Turning back to Wagner, Becker, and Lina, the ambassador said, "Please meet Alex Larsson." After the introductions were made, they all moved to one of the cement benches along the pathway and sat down with Alex positioned in the middle in order for everyone to hear him.

Alex began, "Since the Nazis are looking for two men and one woman, it's imperative we split you up. You will travel on the same transportation at the same time but appearing not to be together. We decided our best bet was to get you to Istanbul. The train ride from Zurich to Istanbul takes approximately ten hours. However, after you leave Switzerland, the train travels through enemy territory. Needless to say, you will be wearing civilian clothing. It's best to stay neutral in unfriendly countries."

After pausing for a few moments, Alex continued, "When you arrive in Istanbul, one of our agents will meet you at the train station. He knows what you look like and he'll find you. The code he will use is, 'Particularly nasty weather we're having.' He will drive you to the dock and get you aboard a ship. The next leg of your journey, from Istanbul to Lisbon, will take an estimated six days by ship. That, of course, depends on the weather. There's a U.S. military base in Portugal. They will be expecting you and will return you to the States."

"That sounds easy enough," Becker said nonchalantly.

"Don't kid yourself," Alex said. "Nothing worth doing ever comes easy."

"With that in mind," Wagner interjected, "what kind of opposition can we expect?"

"Hopefully, none. However, that's nothing we can anticipate, or even plan for. It's much like the weather. Even though it sounds easy, a risk is always present. We've had good results using this plan in the past. However, during wartime everything can change on a dime. We can't guarantee anything."

"That's fair enough," Becker said trying to hide his uneasiness.

Alex continued, "My team is ready to go. Tomorrow morning, one of our buses will come by the embassy and take you to Zurich where you'll board the train. As soon as you arrive at the train station in Zurich, split up. Members of our team will have all of you under constant surveillance." Everyone sat in silence, apparently digesting the anticipated departure.

Finally, Wagner said, "Thank you and thank your team for all your help."

"No, thank you," Alex said. "The three of you undertook an extremely dangerous mission. You're the heroes." Then, looking at Lina he added, "And heroine. You've saved countless lives by destroying the ammunition depot and disrupting the Nazi war machine. The Allies owe you a debt of gratitude."

Becker looked down at his feet, "Not me," he said. "I'm ashamed to admit it, but I'm no hero. I was scared half to death the whole time, and still am." Then looking at Wagner, he added, "Wagner's courage reinforces me…"

Wagner coughed. "If it's any consolation, I, too, was scared half to death. What's that old saying, 'You never know how strong you are until being strong is the only choice you have.' If you'll remember, you kept me and my big mouth from getting us killed a couple of times."

Becker smiled, "Yeah. There is that," he said. However, his smile didn't reach his eyes.

After an awkward silence, Alex said, "Heroes aren't immune to fear. It's how they handle the fear that makes them heroes. My definition of courage is the act of doing something you're afraid to do." He then looked at the ambassador, "Now, about that bourbon…"

Retiring to the ambassador's office, over glasses of bourbon, the five coconspirators engaged in lively conversation involving a pseudo escape plan. Alex had designed the false plan exactly opposite the real one. Wagner, Becker, and Lina bombarded him with questions to make the false plan look legitimate. They were purposely vague to make repetition an impossibility. Their deftness was having its intended result. Their ebb and flow would have Hilda and her comrades running in circles. Diversion was their strategy and they didn't *think* it would work. They *knew* it would!

Hilda was in her room with her ear pressed against the receiver. She relished imagining how she would be honored when the saboteurs were captured. Her shrewdness would be rewarded. The sweeping winds of betrayal did not bother her in the least. Being an ardent supporter of Hitler and the Nazi cause, the end justified the means. Who got trampled in the process was of no consequence— not now, not ever!

Chapter Ten

Implementation

The next morning, just as promised, a bus stopped at the entrance of the embassy. Wagner, Becker, and Lina were waiting in the foyer. The ambassador had Hans prepare each of them a sack lunch which they stored in their backpacks. Hilda watched from the top of the stairs as the three vagabonds boarded the bus. She was almost giddy fantasizing about how important she would soon become and gloating over the humiliation the three targets would soon be experiencing. Vanity blocked any thought as to the ambassador's fate once his complicity was revealed.

The ambassador stood in his open office doorway waiting for his guests to depart. From his vantage point, he was able to see Hilda at the top of the stairs. Her demeanor and her appearing at the top of the stairs at the exact moment of their guests' departure was unusual behavior. It didn't go unnoticed by the ambassador. *How could she know when they were leaving unless she was listening to our conversation last evening. Hilda is the traitor!* The ambassador was saddened as he remembered how much trust he had put in his housekeeper. *The*

Nazis will probably exact their pound of flesh when they discover they've been duped. But, before it's over, I want her to know that I know what she is. I'll find a way...until then, I must keep up my end of the pretense. How can I build an alibi and turn the tables? The death knell would be hers, not mine!

• • •

It was an hour's ride from the embassy to Zurich. The bus took them directly to the train station where they split up. When they entered, Wagner, Becker, and Lina found the waiting area swarming with people of every nationality. They witnessed several arguments among the ill-tempered travelers who were standing in line waiting to purchase tickets. The offenders were quickly escorted out of the station house by guards. Luckly, the underground had provided Wagner, Becker, and Lina with tickets to Istanbul, so they avoided having to wait in line. Becker and Lina followed Wagner's lead and snaked their way through the crowd, going directly to the train platform.

The platform was poorly lit by a string of bare overhead light bulbs. It smelled of coal smoke and unwashed bodies. Families huddled together and children clung tightly to their mother's skirts. The platform was as crowded as the waiting area, and with no safety railing, Wagner feared someone might fall onto the tracks. He became anxious as he strained his neck trying to keep Becker and Lina in sight. However, with so many people milling about, Wagner was pushed and pulled in all directions and soon lost visual contact with them.

When an ear-splitting shrill signaled the approaching train, frightened children started wailing. Apparently eager to secure a seat on the train, the excited throng pushed forward vying for position. The entire platform was bedlam. Wagner was soon caught up in the press of bodies rushing toward the train's open doors. Once aboard, Wagner was able to break free of the throng. He deftly walked through the cars hoping to locate Becker and Lina. When he didn't immediately spot them, he feared they had missed the train.

The train's whistle sounded again, and with a sudden jerk, it was underway. Its departure was so rocky, Wagner had to steady himself by holding onto the back of the seats as he weaved his way through looking for his companions. Not finding them, and now out of options, Wagner reluctantly gave up and began to look for a seat. He hoped Becker and Lina were somewhere on the train but he was not optimistic. The whole episode was nerve racking.

A young woman, apparently noticing Wagner coming down the aisle, moved a boy who looked to be about three from a seat and across from her and offered the seat to Wagner. Wagner thanked her and sat down. The woman, apparently the boy's mother, held the child on her lap. Once situated, Wagner leaned his head against the back of his seat and stared out the window as the countryside whizzed by. With a ten-hour train ride in front of him, Wagner's eyes soon closed, and the rocking of the train lured him into an exhausted sleep.

A few hours later, Wagner was awakened by a crying child. For a few moments, he couldn't remember where he was. Then it dawned on him and he sat up straighter. Looking out the window, he asked the young mother, "Where are we?"

Repositioning the child on her lap, the mother said, "About halfway to Istanbul."

The child continued to cry, "Hungry, Mommy, hungry."

Now fully awake, Wagner remembered the sack lunch the chef had prepared for the journey. He removed it from his rucksack. Inside was a sandwich, cookies, and an apple. He took the apple and gave the rest to the boy's mother. When she hesitated, Wagner urged her to take the food. "For the boy," he said.

The mother gave him a weak smile, and as tears slid down her cheeks, she whispered, "Danke."

Thinking the mother might be embarrassed, and not wanting to prolong the exchange, Wagner bit into the apple and turned his attention back to the window. After eating part of the sandwich and a cookie, the boy fell asleep in his mother's arms. Glancing at the slumbering child, Wagner couldn't help but think, *What kind of world will you have? God help us all.*

• • •

When they detrained in Istanbul, Wagner faced the same crush of travelers heading for the train's exits. Once on the platform, he again began looking for Becker and Lina. That was when he noticed the menacing and dark Nazi officer standing at a large window inside the waiting area overlooking the platform. He seemed to be surveilling the new arrivals. *Is he looking for us?*

As he stood on the platform trying to decide what to do, the child he had sat across from on the train became fussy. Reaching up to his mother, he began to wail, "Up, Mommy, up!" demanding she carry him.

Apparently, not wanting to make a scene, the mother picked the child up and he quieted down. Watching the exchange, it was obvious to Wagner that the mother could not manage their luggage and carry the child. Wagner seized the opportunity.

Hoping they would look like a family, Wagner asked the mother if he could carry her luggage into the station house. She gratefully accepted his offer.

When they entered the station house, Wagner turned his head away from the Nazi who was still standing at the window. Wagner walked with the mother and child through the crowd to the exit and onto the walkway in front of the train station. To his relief, the mother was immediately greeted by an elderly couple who had apparently been waiting for her. They thanked Wagner for helping their daughter, and picking up her luggage, they escorted her and child to a car parked across the street.

Suddenly, feeling exposed as he stood watching them drive off, Wagner turned back toward the station house where the crowd would at least afford him more cover. However, before he could enter, a car pulled to the curb. The driver leaned over, and opening the passenger door said, "Particularly nasty weather we're having." It took a moment for Wagner to connect. Then it suddenly hit him, *The code! That's the code!* Wagner bent and looked inside the van. When he saw Becker and Lina in the rear seats, he breathed a sigh of relief. The realization was jolting and his expression was like the hungry child when he was given the cookie.

Without much ado, the driver said, "Get in! I'm

your ride to the pier."

Wagner wasted no time jumping into the front seat. As soon as he closed the passenger door, from the backseat, Becker clasped Wagner's shoulder. Relief was evident in his voice as he said, "We were worried about you."

Too emotional to speak, Wagner squeezed Becker's hand and turned to look at him. Lina leaned forward and reached out to Wagner. As she did so, Wagner had a clear view out of the rear window of the vehicle. He saw the Nazi officer he previously noticed in the station house pointing in their direction. He was getting into a military vehicle. *They're looking for us.*

"I think we're being tailed," Wagner said as he turned back.

"How's that?" the driver asked, as he maneuvered the car into the oncoming traffic.

Wagner explained his suspicions regarding the Nazi officer.

"Hmm," the driver said. "The Nazis have no legitimate authority here since Turkey is a neutral country. However, they are bullies and the population offers little resistance to their demands." After a pause, the driver continued, "I know your histories and I, too, refuse to be bullied. There are two pistols in that compartment," he gestured to the glove box, "in case we need them. Be careful, they're loaded."

Wagner opened the compartment and asked as he retrieved the weapons, "What's your name?"

"Lars," answered the driver who kept anxiously glancing in the rearview mirror.

Wagner extracted the weapons and handed one back over his shoulder to Becker.

"This is my neck of the woods," Lars said. "I know a short cut to the pier." Glancing out of the rearview mirror, he shouted, "Hold on!" and took a sharp turn off the highway onto a narrow unpaved access road. Again, looking into the rearview mirror, he said, "I was hoping they'd miss the turn, but they're still on our tail."

Examining the weapon, Wagner said, "Okay, Lars. You do the drivin', we'll do the shootin'…if need be."

• • •

The access road was so dry, clouds of dust bellowed out from behind Lars' car obscuring them from their pursuers. About ten minutes into the chase, Lars once again made a sharp turn across an easement and onto the highway. There was a sudden cacophony of honking horns and screeching tires as drivers maneuvered their vehicles to avoid colliding with Lars' car. With his hands against the dashboard, Wagner braced himself and looked back just in time to see the Nazi vehicle whiz past the place where they turned off.

"Good job! They missed the turn," Wagner said to Lars. With a broad smile, he added, "Where'd you learn to drive, Indianapolis Speedway?"

Lars just grinned.

• • •

Shortly after getting back onto the highway, Lars said, "We're getting close to the pier. The name of the ship you'll be boarding is *Yoleu*—translates to *Wayfarer*. She's registered as a cargo ship. Don't let her dilapidated exterior fool you, she's top of the line. Her owner, Captain Kaya, uses the disguise to dissuade the Nazis. *Yoleu* is equipped with enough armor to sink almost any predator. So far, he's been lucky. The captain's theory is, she already looks too much like a wreck to waste a torpedo on."

That is, unless someone wants to use her for target practice, Becker thought.

"Will there be other passengers on board?" Lina asked.

"Probably. Since it's a six-day trip, I assume Kaya will want a full boat to make the trip worthwhile and legitimate." Lars pulled into the parking area close to the bustling dock. "Grab your gear and come with me," he said as he stepped out of the car and surveyed the crowd. Nothing looked suspicious.

Lars' three passengers wasted no time joining him. They were eager to stretch their legs. There were several ships at anchor, and the dock was swarming with people of many different nationalities. They chatted and quarreled in many different languages as they searched for their ship. Shirtless stevedores with bulging, sweat-covered muscles carried cargo down the gangplanks and loaded their freight onto waiting trucks. The stevedores, even laden with their burdens, were adept at dodging the menagerie of people milling about looking lost and confused.

"Stay close to me," Lars cautioned. "I know where *Yoleu* is docked." After a few minutes of shouldering their way through the mayhem, Lars pointed to a ship in the distance. "There she is," he said.

When they closed the gap, it was obvious the three refugees weren't impressed with the ship. "You sure that thing can float?" Becker asked, his voice laced with concern.

"Remember, I warned you. And yes, to answer your question, she can float," Lars said. "You needn't worry about her seaworthiness."

"That's reassuring," Wagner muttered.

"I'll come with you and introduce you to the

captain," Lars said.

The captain was in the cabin when he apparently noticed Lars and the three travelers coming up the gangplank. He came out to greet them. "Ahoy!" he said with a broad smile."

"Captain Kaya, permission to come aboard," Lars said as he executed a smart salute. "These are your three Lisbon passengers."

"Welcome aboard," Kaya said and gestured for them all to come aboard. Always feeling exposed when they were out in the open, they wasted no time boarding. All the while, Lars was on full alert scrutinizing the passengers to make sure there were no unwanted passengers boarding or unsavory characters lurking in the shadows.

After Lars made the introductions, Kaya said, "It's almost time for the noon meal. I'll have the seaman show you to your quarters and you can freshen up before lunch." Kaya gestured to a young seaman standing close by. "Paco, show our guests to their quarters."

"Aye, aye, Captain," Paco said. Then to the passengers, "Please follow me."

The captain and Lars watched as Wagner, Becker, and Lina followed the seaman down the passageway. The passengers staggered, awkwardly trying to keep upright as the ship swayed with the tide.

"They'll soon get the hang of it," Kaya said, and looking at Lars, he opened the door to the cabin. "Come in and tell me what's been going on. I've been out to sea for weeks."

The two men sipped a glass of scotch as Lars brought the captain up to date on the war effort and what the underground had been doing. The captain roared with laughter when Lars told him about *Operation Juggernaut.*

"You mean my passengers, those three scalawags, outsmarted the Nazi army?" Kaya said.

"Yep, that they did. They blew hell out of the tunnel going through the Needles, putting a fairly big crimp in the Nazi war machine."

"Well, I'll be damned," Kaya said as he rubbed his chin. Then holding up his glass, offered a toast. "Here's to the bold from morning 'til night. Here's to the people with courage to fight. The courage to fight and the courage to live. The courage to learn, to love, and forgive."

"Here, here," Lars responded. "That's pretty profound. Did you make that up?"

"Me? Naw. Hemmingway gets the credit."

Setting his glass on his desk, Kaya said, "I suppose the Nazis are frantically searching for the culprits."

"That they are!" Lars replied. "Because of the

magnitude of the damage the explosion caused and the effect it had on the Nazi war effort, I'm sure there's a wide sweep underway to catch the saboteurs. I wouldn't trust anyone. The Jerrys are frantic and have spies everywhere. They would probably give a fortune to anyone for turning them in."

"Hell, yes, There's no doubt about it! That little escapade most likely cost some officers dearly," Kaya said. He held up the bottle and looked at Lars.

Slapping his palms against his thighs, Lars stood and said, "As tempting as it is to slay the afternoon chatting with you, I better not. Thanks anyway, I should get back to Istanbul. No telling what surprises are waiting for me there."

Kaya stood and walked Lars to the gangplank. "You, my friend, watch your back. You're in an extremely volatile position."

"No more than you," Lars responded. "We couldn't do what we do without your help. It's patriots like you who are unflinchingly helping the Allies win this war."

The two men exchanged bear hugs, and as Lars stepped onto the gangplank, Kaya's eyes narrowed as he said, "Until next time, you take care."

Turning back, Lars replied, "And you as well." He knew Kaya's admonition was more than a cliché and that Kaya was familiar with the route and more importantly, formidable when it came to outsmarting a predictable war machine bent on evening the score.

Chapter Eleven

Navigation

Although the *Yoleu's* exterior was junkyard ugly, much to the surprise of Wagner, Becker, and Lina, the interior of the ship was neat and clean. The massive ship masqueraded as something she wasn't, like a chameleon. Wagner and Lina took to sailing like professionals. However, Becker succumbed to seasickness. He stayed in his cabin suffering from dizziness and profuse sweating. He was weak and had severe bouts of nausea and vomiting. Concerned about Becker's condition, Wagner immediately sought help from the ship's doctor.

"Sounds like a case of seasickness. It's not uncommon to experience seasickness if you're not used to sailing," the doctor told Wagner after Wagner explained Becker's symptoms. "Even seasoned sailors can get sick in extremely rough weather." The doctor prepared a mixture of ginger root and water. "Make him drink this and eat a few crackers," he said. "When he's strong enough, take him up to the deck. The fresh air will help."

Following the doctor's orders, Wagner encouraged Becker to drink the ginger root concoction. Amazingly, the cure worked and Becker gradually became stronger. The second day at sea, although still weak, Becker appeared to be recuperating. Wagner and Lina accompanied him to the deck where they stood at the railing breathing in the fresh sea air. Becker seemed to revive even more.

When the three tired of watching ponderous waves and the endless expanse of an empty sea, they read old ship longs, diaries of Kaya's predecessors, and old books destined for extinction. They were captivated by Kaya's diary entries recalling encounters with both nature and man. He had dodged pirates and enemy vessels, including Nazi submarines and destroyers. Kaya had disdain for anything and everything Nazi. Oppression was not in his vernacular.

• • •

In the middle of the night on the third day at sea, the ship's occupants were awakened by an unexpected, violent storm.

Wagner went out onto the passageway where he encountered sailors rushing around in a coordinated effort. The wind was so strong, Wagner had a hard time standing up. As he clung to the wet railing, he asked one of the sailors as the sailor rushed past, "What's going on?"

"Looks like a hurricane," the sailor said, and

pushed past Wagner.

"What?" Wagner shouted. The sailor was gone before Wagner could ask any more questions. The rain was coming down in torrents and huge waves like never before rocked the ship. The howling wind was deafening and cut right through him. Feeling helpless, Wagner watched the sailor try to balance himself as he staggered down the passageway.

Suddenly, Lina and Becker were at Wagner's side, hanging onto the railing for dear life. Another sailor was rapidly approaching. Upon coming face to face with him, Lina asked, "How bad is it?" Her voice trembled with fear.

"We may be in a hurricane," another sailor said. "At the very least, we've been hit head-on by a sudden violent storm, that might damage the hull. If the ship takes on too much water it'll sink. Pray that doesn't happen."

"Oh, no!" Lina shouted, panic in her voice. "What can we do?" she asked out of desperation.

"Prepare for the worst and hope for the best!" the sailor shouted. "You three, come with me. You can help get the lifeboats ready to launch."

Lina paled. *Lifeboats! Is it really that bad?*

A few of the sailors were already removing the covering from the lifeboats when the trio arrived. They had to squeeze past a group of the ship's passengers standing together on the deck watching the activity. Terror was written on the passengers' faces. One of the women was so distraught, she was wringing her hands. Other passengers huddled together, most still clad in their nightclothes.

As Wagner and Becker helped the sailors untie the lifeboats, preparing them to launch, an earsplitting alarm sounded. Already unnerved and filled with dread, some of the women screamed, adding to the commotion and utter consternation.

"That's the abandon ship signal," one of the sailors shouted. "We must be in big trouble." Wasting no time, he motioned to the group of passengers waiting in the passageway, including Wagner, Becker, and Lina, "All of you, get into the boat, and we'll lower it. Hurry! We've no time to spare!"

"How about the rest of you?" Becker asked as he clambered aboard the lifeboat.

The sailor either didn't hear the question or chose to ignore it. Two other sailors assisted him, and they lowered the boat into the ocean. The boat descended slowly down the side of the ship, banging against the hull as the wind continued to rage. It was a short trip, but a horrific one. The sailors stood at the railing watching, and as soon as the boat hit the water, the sailors released the rope sling from the lifeboat and pulled the ropes back up to the deck.

The sea was so rough, the lifeboat rocked precariously as the waves lifted it and slammed it back down. The stormy sea carried the rudderless vessel away from the ship. The waves were so high and the rain so heavy, the passengers, twelve in all, including Wagner, Becker, and Lina, were soon soaking wet. The torrent of rain blocked their view, and they couldn't see beyond their boat to determine if there were other lifeboats in the water or even if the ship was still afloat.

Wagner cringed when he realized they were on their own. He didn't know much about sailing or what to do when calamity struck. When he looked around at the other passengers, he doubted if any of them did either. They all appeared to be frightened and confused. They were at the mercy of the elements.

• • •

The storm raged on through the night, tossing the lifeboat around in the ocean like it was a child's toy. The noise the storm created was so loud, they found it impossible to communicate without screaming at each other. It was too dark to examine the inside of the lifeboat to determine what supplies, if any, were provided. The survivors, hunkering down trying to stay warm, sat on the wooden seats, six on each side of the craft. Although it seemed like an eternity, in reality it was only a few hours before the wind and rain gradually subsided as the storm dissipated. When dawn finally broke over the horizon, Wagner took charge.

"Each of you take a look around your immediate area. There should be containers of water and other life-sustaining articles on board."

After a thorough search, all they came up with was four oars, a small metal bailer bucket, a first aid kit, some fishing gear, and a knife. No drinking water.

It was still drizzling rain, so upon pondering their plight and seeking solutions, Wagner said, "First of all, we're going to need drinking water. Catch as much rain as you can in that bucket." He then asked, without much hope, "Anyone have a compass?"

Much to Wagner's surprise, Otto, one of the men said, "I do!"

"You do?"

"Yes. My watch has a small compass on its face." Otto unstrapped the watch and handed it to Wagner. "I hope the water didn't ruin it," he said.

Wagner took the watch and studied it for a moment. When he saw the second hand moving, he shouted, "It's working!" Taking a deep breath, he addressed his fellow survivors. "I'm not going to kid you, our situation is desperate. However, we do have a fighting chance. My friend," Wagner pointed to Becker, "and I were trained by the greatest fighting force in the world, the U.S. military. We received in-depth instruction in survival skills. Nothing was sugar coated, our lives depended on us being equipped to face adverse situations and come out alive on the other side.

"These are the cold, hard facts," Wagner continued, then paused and looked around. The look on the passengers' faces caused him concern. Hoping to avoid all out panic, he gave them some hope. "We can live three weeks without food as long as we have water. We can only last three days without water. Even though drinking rainwater is not recommended, since we're in survival mode, we have no choice. We'll collect rainwater in that bucket and deal with the consequences after we're safe. With water we can last two to three weeks, even without food. That's what we're facing."

Holding up the watch, Wagner pressed on, "We're fortunate to have two necessities, a compass and oars. We'll take turns rowing. Maybe with some luck we can catch a fish or two. I hear raw fish isn't so bad." Wagner's audience sat transfixed. It was apparent they were relieved that someone who knew what he was doing was taking charge.

Gazing out over the seemingly endless expanse of ocean, Wagner continued, "All I know is that we're somewhere on the Mediterranean. No way of telling how far we were carried off course by the storm. If we keep our heads and move in one direction, we'll eventually hit land. Hopefully, it will be a friendly nation." Wagner paused for a few moments. "If anyone has a better plan, let's hear it."

One of the men held up his hand. "I'm Father Ryan," he said. "I'd like to lead us in a prayer and ask for His assistance in guiding us to that friendly nation."

All the passengers bowed their heads, some made the sign of the cross as Father Ryan prayed. "Dear Lord, thank You for sparing us. Please continue to bless us as we embark on this perilous journey. Continue to guide us in Your ways. Grant us wisdom and courage equal to that of Your disciples as You led them through dangerous situations such as what we're now facing. We pray that You keep us under the canopy of Your divine love and protection. Also, we pray that You help the Allies prevail and not let evil be victorious. We ask this in the name of Your Precious Son, Jesus Christ. Amen."

"Amen," came the response from everyone on the boat. No atheists in fox holes or boats adrift.

· · ·

Because of the lingering stormy weather left in the wake of the hurricane, the boat people were able to fill the bucket with rainwater the first day. Using all four oars, they took turns rowing in teams of four, even the women participated. They rowed day and night to keep from drifting.

One of the women was overheard gasping as she rowed, "Go… Good way to get much needed exercise."

Another one responded, "That's one way to look at it."

To keep spirits up, they sang hymns and popular songs of the day. Everyone seemed to be committed to their survival and did their job without complaint.

To keep from drifting off course, although Wagner didn't know where they were or where they were going, he constantly checked the compass to make sure they moved in one direction to avoid going around in circles. The watch face was illuminated, so he was able to check it even during the night.

· · ·

The morning of the second day at sea, the boat people were surprised when a good-sized fish miscalculated and jumped into their boat. Acting quickly, one of the men slipped off a shoe, and whacked the fish. It flopped a few times, then lay still. Looking at his kill, he said to no one in particular, "I killed it, you clean it!"

Two of the men cleaned the fish and sliced it into twelve portions. As they ate the raw fish, someone said, "Father Ryan, could you use your connections and see if you can get us some loaves to go with this fish?" The boat people, including Father Ryan, had a hearty laugh.

Wiping tears from his eyes, Father Ryan said, "Don't think I'm that well connected. However, if you don't believe in miracles, there's a logical explanation for the fish coming aboard. I noticed when Mr. Wagner was manipulating the watch, the sun reflected off the watch's face. The fish must've thought the bright, flashing light was a tasty morsel flying around and jumped for it." After a pause, he added, "However, we know who's in charge and who gets the credit. Thank you, Lord."

• • •

It was obvious on the third day at sea everyone was getting weary. They were showing signs of exhaustion. They had no cover from the oppressive sun. Their strength, endurance, and vigor were diminishing. They hadn't had anything to eat since the fish the day before and now the rain was sparse and they were running low on water. Although they used the fish entrails for bait, they couldn't catch another fish, not even a nibble. Wagner attributed that to the constant splashing of the oars and the movement of the boat which scared the fish away.

Suddenly, Maxine, one of the women, shouted, "I can't take it any longer!" and she flung her legs over the side of the boat. Before she could jettison herself into the ocean, Jake, the man seated behind her, dropped his oar and grabbed her by the arm. Others jumped up to help subdue her. They dragged her back into the boat as she screamed and fought. Once aboard, she dropped onto her seat and began to weep.

Retrieving a shawl and wrapping it around Maxine's shoulders, Louise, an elderly woman said, "Now, now, dearie, it's going to be alright."

"You don't know that!" Maxine shouted. She tore the shawl from around her shoulders and shoved it back into Louise's arms.

"And you don't know it's not!" came the reply from someone midship. "We have enough to contend with without worrying about you and your craziness!"

Before the entire boat erupted into chaos, Wagner stood and shouted over the din, "Attention! Everyone, calm down! I have an announcement to make."

Silence fell over the boat and everyone turned their attention toward Wagner. "I didn't want to tell you earlier and give you false hope, but I sense the flow seems to now be moving with us. That's an indication we're getting close to land."

"You're just saying that!" Maxine screamed, still distraught and disgusted with everyone and everything.

"No, I'm not—" Wagner began to protest.

Before Wagner could finish his sentence, from the stern of the boat, Becker shouted, "Look, lady, you're causing chaos and panic. You calm down or I'll personally feed you to the fish."

That was so out of character for Becker, an amazed Wagner looked back at him with a big smile. The rest of the boat applauded their approval. Maxine sank lower in her seat, all the fight had gone out of her.

• • •

With renewed vigor and hope, the oarsmen began rowing at a faster clip. Wagner didn't want to dissuade them. He didn't know if they were ten, fifteen, or even fifty miles from land so he let them cling to their hope and exert their energy.

The day melted into night and they took turns rowing; the mood gradually changed from gleeful to solemn.

Becker made his way aft and sat down beside Wagner. "Any guess about how far it is to land?"

"Not really," Wagner admitted. "In fact, I made

that story up. I thought if they had some hope, they'd be better off. One Maxine is enough!"

"You're a genius," said Becker. "It sounded legit to me. I thought you knew what you were talking about." After a pause, he asked, "What happens if land doesn't appear and soon?"

"I'll probably be the fish bait." Then standing, Wagner said, "It's my turn at the oars. Keep your fingers crossed." He was grateful he was called a genius and not a con artist.

Both physical and mental exhaustion took their toll and after Wagner took his turn rowing, he curled up on his bench and fell into a dreamless sleep. As the sun came up, he was awakened by cheering and shouting, and for an instant he forgot where he was. Becker was soon by his side, "You did it, buddy. Look!" and when Becker pointed, Wagner followed his finger. "Land!" Becker shouted.

"What?" Wagner mumbled and stood to get a better look. They were close enough to see waves breaking on the shore and buildings in the distance. Wagner sank back down and covered his face with his hands. "Thank you, Heavenly Father. Thank you," He whispered.

Becker sat down beside Wagner. "Any idea where we are?"

"Nope. Let's just hope it's friend, not foe."

Chapter Twelve

Trepidation

When they approached the shoreline, Wagner cautioned the boat people to remain silent. "We don't know where we are. We could be in unfriendly territory so let's not announce our arrival."

As soon as the boat was in shallow waters, the men got out and pulled it ashore. As soon as it was secure, they helped the women step out onto the beach. Having sat for so long, all were stiff and awkward and stumbled in the soft sand. Looking heavenward, Father Ryan said a silent prayer thanking God for guiding them ashore.

• • •

Because they could see buildings in the distance as they neared the shore, they knew they were close to a town, and more importantly, close to civilization.

Wagner motioned for everyone to gather around. Addressing his shipmates, he said, "I don't know if we landed on friendly soil or not. Until we find out for sure, we'll take every precaution and assume it's not."

"Do you think we landed in Portugal?" Father

Ryan asked.

"Not sure where we are, Father. Our means of navigation was less than state of the art and we could have drifted off course to some degree." Wagner put his hands on his hips and looked around, "At least we we're on land."

Becker, standing and listening to the exchange between Wagner and Father Ryan, said, "I have a suggestion."

"Let's hear it," Wagner quickly replied.

"Suppose we send a scout into the town to find out where we are before we all go blundering in, only to find out we're in enemy territory or worse yet, at the mercy of headhunters."

"Great idea. However, I think headhunters live in huts, not buildings, so cross that one off your list. By the way, are you volunteering?" Wagner asked.

"Yes," Becker said without hesitation. He stood and brushed sand from his clothes.

"Not so fast. Remember, we're a team? I'm going with you. However, I think we can all move closer to the populated area but keep out of sight until we find out where we are," Wagner warned. "Anyone object?"

No one objected.

Wagner continued, "There's no way of knowing if we've been detected, so we'll assume we haven't.

Since the beach is surrounded by large rocky areas and dense vegetation, it'll be easy to stay out of sight."

The ragtag group, infused with renewed hope and excitement, lined up and quietly walked to a spot close to the town. When they were near enough to hear the sounds of traffic, Wagner held up a hand signaling that they stop. "This is close enough," he said. "Becker and I will go the rest of the way alone." He then parted the overgrowth with his hands, and as he peered through at what lay ahead, he added, "Stay out of sight until we get back!"

"What if you don't get back?" Father Ryan asked.

"Guess you'll know it's not too safe…" Wagner replied.

Before they took two steps, Lina jumped up. "Wait," she said. "I'm going with you."

"It may not be safe—" Becker began.

"I don't care. Lest you forget, I'm part of the team," Lina said defiantly as she jutted her chin. "Besides, traveling with a woman makes you look less aggressive."

"Oh, for cryin' out loud, we don't have time to argue," Wagner groaned. "Come on," and gestured to Lina to catch up.

• • •

The trio traveled in silence until they reached the outskirts of the town. There, under cover of the brush, they watched and listened. They were close to an open-air marketplace. The plaza was teaming with a variety of shoppers wearing garments native to their various countries. The venders touted their ware in a variety of languages, so it was difficult to determine what the local language was. Having noticed many of the men were wearing a fez, and knowing the fez was headwear indigenous to Morocco, Wagner surmised they must have missed Portugal, and drifted farther south, coming ashore in Morocco.

After watching for a few minutes, Wagner decided it would be safe enough to enter the marketplace. "You stay here until I find out where we are," he said, and slipped from their hide before anyone could argue with him. Becker and Lina watched as he approached the nearest vendor. Using German, he asked the proprietor, "What city is this?"

Obviously, foreigners were not rare in this place as the vender didn't seem surprised by the question. Without looking up, he said, "Tangier."

Knowing Tangier was in northern Morocco across the Strait of Gibraltar which separates Portugal from North Africa, his assumption that they had drifted south was correct. He thanked the vendor and hurried back to where Becker and Lina were waiting.

"We're in Tangier, Morocco. We missed Portugal, but Morocco is a neutral country and the melting pot of almost every nationality. I think we'll be safe here."

Upon hearing the news, Becker sagged and breathed a sigh. It was evident he was relieved they were in a neutral country. "Let's go get the others," he said and stood.

"Wait. I first want to see if there's an American embassy close by," Wagner said.

"Okay, I'll go get the others while you find out about the embassy. That'll save time." Then looking around, Becker asked, "Where shall we meet?"

"It'll take you about two hours to make the roundtrip. Since we don't know the layout, let's meet right here in approximately two hours," Wagner suggested. He removed the watch from his wrist and handed it to Becker. Then pointing to a clock in a tower across the plaza, said, "I'll use that one."

Lina had quietly been listening to the exchange. Annoyed at being ignored, she tilted her head and said, "Pardon me, but I thought I was a part of this team." Her sarcasm did not go unnoticed.

"Of course, you are. You'll come with me,"

Wagner said realizing their blunder. "We may appear to be less threatening if we look like a couple."

Becker chuckled to himself. Good save!

"Thank you! I'm glad to be of assistance," Lina snapped.

Trying to further cover their *faux pas*, Wagner stated, "We could not have completed this mission without you. Not only are you a member of the team, but you were the most essential element. Without your help, the operation would've been a dismal failure."

Looking sheepish, Becker offered, "You deserve a Congressional Medal of Honor. Your assistance probably saved thousands of lives… including mine and Wagner's."

"That's right, Lina." After a pause, Wagner added, "If we get outta this, how will we ever be able to repay you?"

With measured words, Lina replied, "I want to live in America." After a brief pause, she asked, "Can you help me?"

"I think that can be arranged through the immigration process. We'll do our best," Becker promised.

"Thank you. That's all I can expect."

• • •

The trio split up and went separate ways. Becker headed back to rejoin the rest of the boat people. Wagner and Lina strolled through the marketplace posing as shoppers. They stopped every so often to examine some article on display, just as couples would do.

One of the vendors took particular interest in the couple. "You like silk?" he said to Lina as they strolled past his kiosk.

Not knowing how to avoid the question, Lina replied, "Why yes, I like silk."

Holding up a scarf, the vendor said, "Nice item. Come from China," and he handed it to Lina.

"Yes, it is nice, but—"

"Special price for beautiful lady," the vendor said with a broad smile.

"Ah, thank you but I —"

"Oh, you hurt feelings. You take as gift, okay?" the vendor pleaded, handing the scarf back to Lina.

Lina reluctantly accepted the gift. "Thank you," she said. Then as an afterthought, she asked, "American Embassy?"

The vendor nodded and pointed. "Around corner, you will see." He then turned his attention to other customers who were showing interest in his merchandise.

As they walked away, Wagner said to Lina,

"Don't know what that was all about, but I'm suspicious of everyone and everything anymore."

Lina didn't reply. It appeared she, too, was bewildered, and she stuffed the scarf into a pocket.

• • •

Wagner and Lina casually walked toward the corner the vendor had indicated. When they turned, they saw a beautiful large, two-story, sand-colored stucco building. The courtyard was fitted with tilework and marble. The entrance was an arch similar to the ones used on mosques. It was protected by a covered portico. A waist-high stucco fence surrounded the building and a sign posted at the entrance identified it as the American Embassy.

Lina grabbed Wagner's hand, "We made it!" she exclaimed.

"I think so." Wagner looked up and down the street but couldn't see the tower clock from where they were standing. "It must be getting close to time to meet Becker. Let's head back," he said. "We can find out from the Americans if there are other embassies or safe havens we're not aware of."

When they returned to the meeting place, Becker and the boat people were waiting. Wagner noticed everyone looked anxious so he immediately said, "We have located the American Embassy. It's a short distance from here."

"Great!" Becker said with a broad smile.

"How about us non-Americans?" Otto asked in a desperate tone.

"Any embassy can protect and help refugees from other countries who are in immediate danger and seeking shelter. Rest assured the American ambassador will help you even though you're not American citizens," Becker replied.

"How can you be so sure?" Otto asked still perplexed.

"We were so informed in bootcamp—in case we were ever in a position where we had to seek the help of an embassy." Then turning to Wagner, Becker said, "Lead the way!"

Apparently satisfied with Becker's answer, the boat people fell in behind Becker and Wagner. After a short walk, they approached the American Embassy. All twelve refugees crossed the patio and crowded in under the portico. Wagner rang the doorbell.

Moments later a stern-looking tall, slender man opened the door. He was dressed in a white, long-sleeved, flowing gown-like garment that was slit up both sides. The garment was worn over white pants that fit close to his ankles. He had a white turban wrapped around his head and a neatly trimmed dark beard. His olive skin and dark features were a stark contrast to the white clothing he wore. If he was stunned to see twelve people standing on the portico, it didn't show. "How may I help you?" he asked in perfect English.

"We're refugees seeking asylum," Wagner replied as he sized up the greeter. Skepticism made him leery and apprehensive.

Still unfazed by the sudden appearance of twelve rag-tag wayfarers on his doorstep, the man stepped aside and beckoned them in. "Please wait. I'll let the Ambassador know we have refugees," he said and vanished into the interior of the embassy.

Moments later, a distinguished-looking gentleman dressed in an American-style business suit, walked toward them with his hand extended. "I'm Ambassador Richard Edmondson," he said as he surveyed the group.

After introductions were made, Wagner said, "Mr. Ambassador, I'm the self-appointed spokesman for our group. May I have a private conference with you?"

Looking puzzled, the ambassador replied, "Absolutely, I'll have Salman provide quarters and have Umar, our chef, prepare a meal." Salman, the same individual who answered the door, was standing nearby and quickly approached. The ambassador said, "Salman, see to the comfort of our guests." Salman bowed and touched his heart, lips, and forehead with his fingertips—a gesture of obedience in the Muslim culture. Then turning to the waiting refugees, he said, "Come with me."

Watching them leave, Ambassador Edmondson said to Wagner, "If you're who I think you are, you have quite a story to tell. Accompany me to my office."

Once they were situated in the ambassador's office, the ambassador said, "You have the floor, let's hear it."

I like this guy, he's definitely not a stuffed shirt. "First, before I begin, Mr. Ambassador, no offense intended, but who do you think I am?" Wagner asked, apparently not wanting to give up too much to a stranger. The encounter with the Nazi spy, Hilda, was still fresh in his mind.

"No offense taken," the ambassador said and offered Wagner a cigarette. Wagner shook his head. The ambassador continued, "We recently received word that there was a major disaster involving an ammunition dump at the base of the Alps on the border between Austria and Germany. It appears two imposters, disguised as German officers, were able to penetrate a highly guarded passageway between Austria and Germany and execute a mission known as *Operation Juggernaut.* When we received the notification approximately a week after the incident, the perpetrators had not yet been captured." At the end of his narration, the Ambassador sat back, and lighting a cigarette, stared at Wagner.

"Okay, you passed the test," Wagner finally said. "Hope you understand my apprehension and distrust…"

"Of course! One cannot be too careful these days."

Feeling more comfortable, Wagner told the story, chapter and verse, of how the three of them happened to wind up on the Ambassador's doorstep.

"Outsmarting the Nazi army is quite a feat. I'll try to make sure you live to tell it to your children and grandchildren."

Wagner laughed. "Never thought about it that way. We felt lucky when we saw the sun rise every day when we were, and still are, on the lam." After a pause, Wagner added, "When we boarded the ship in Istanbul, we were headed for Portugal and the American military base situated there. Is it possible to get Lina to America? She risked her life multiple times and her only request was to be allowed to live in America."

The ambassador wrinkled his brow, apparently in deep thought. He finally said, "There's a daily flight out of Casablanca to the U.S. base at Lajes Field on Terceria Island in Portugal. You'll need exit visas to make the trip. The locals owe me a favor and I think I have enough clout to get it done. I'll see about exit visas for the three of you. We'll turn the other refugees over to their respective embassies for safekeeping." Standing, the ambassador said, "In the meantime, it smells like the chef has cooked up something delicious. Will you join me and the others for the afternoon meal?"

"You bet I will. Haven't had anything to eat other than a slice of raw fish in six days," Wagner said woefully. Just the mention of food was gripping. The three had been surviving on frayed nerves and mass confusion. The scene at sea flashed through his head, and with the mention of food, his anguish quickly dissipated.

"Six days! Amazing. The main meal in Tangier is the noon meal. Come on, let's get you some nourishment."

• • •

Knowing everyone was starving, literally, Father Ryan said a quick prayer thanking God for their deliverance. At the end of the prayer, the dining room erupted in joyful chatter as the refugees dined on a meal consisting of a variety of boiled vegetables, lamb, boiled eggs, and bread.

It was topped off with a dessert of mint tea and Moroccan cookies.

When it looked as though everyone had finished eating, Ambassador Edmondson stood and tapped the side of his glass with a butter knife to get their attention. When the chatter subsided, he said, "It's the custom here in Morocco to take an afternoon siesta. I believe you all have quarters, so I encourage you to join in with our custom and take a nap." Surprise lit up his face, as he wasn't expecting the round of applause he received after making the announcement. Everyone was weary, even Ambassador Edmondson. The grateful guests didn't need any coaxing. Listlessly they stumbled to their assigned quarters and dreamt of a better tomorrow.

Chapter Thirteen

Transportation

Wagner met with the ambassador first thing the following morning while the others slept in. They discussed the different ways to get to Portugal.

"It's a four-hour drive from Tangier to Casablanca. However, there's a night train that runs between the two cities. It takes a little over two hours."

"Which way do you think is the safest?" Wagner asked.

"Hard to say," the ambassador said. "I don't know how many check points you go through if you drive. I'm sure they've beefed up security since the Juggernaut incident and probably added several more check points. Not only was that a blow to their supply chain, but also to their confidence and respect. Having a major facility sabotaged was a bitter pill to swallow. If you're captured, pray for death, as their torture tactics are unspeakable."

Wagner cringed at the thought. "How about the train?" he asked.

"There are advantages to taking the train," the ambassador replied. "For starters, you can split up and not appear to be traveling together. You'd have the coverage of being among other travelers. Plus, you'd be exposed for only two hours, instead of four. Weighing the pros and cons, I'd think I'd opt for the train."

"Your points are well taken, and I agree," Wagner said. "When does the train leave?"

"It leaves every night at nine. However, I still have to obtain the exit visas. In today's climate, exit visas are like gold. They're a must in order to leave the country. However, getting the visas won't be problematic. I have a friend who owes me a favor. Getting the visas will be my priority immediately after breakfast. Plan on leaving this evening. We should keep your departure close to the vest. Tell only your two companions. What's that old saying? *Trust everyone but cut the cards.*"

Wagner smiled and nodded. the ambassador's American colloquialisms made him miss home even more. He was suddenly overcome with homesickness. "In the event I don't have a chance to thank you before we leave, Ambassador Edmondson, I hope you know how much your help means to us. It's obvious you put your life on the line every day. I thank you, for all of us, from the bottom of our hearts."

The ambassador cleared his throat. It was

apparent he was moved by Wagner's words. "You're welcome," he finally said. "However, you're the heroes. It's my honor and privilege to be of service to you." After an awkward moment, the ambassador looked at his watch. "My, look at the time," he said. "We have a big day ahead of us. The others will soon be stumbling out of bed expecting bacon and eggs and the other goodies the chef will be preparing for our honored guests."

Wagner stood and the two men walked to the dining room together.

• • •

After breakfast, the ambassador left the embassy. He had Salman drive him to police headquarters where he met with Chief Iliad Muhammad.

"Ambassador Edmondson! Please come into my office," Muhammad said. "Will you join me in a cup of coffee?"

Remembering how strong the Muslim coffee was, the ambassador said, "No, thank you. I had my quota at breakfast."

"As you wish," Muhammad said, and saluted the ambassador by raising his coffee cup to eye level. "Now, what brings you to my humble establishment?"

"I need three exit visas."

"Oh, and who is it wanting to leave our beautiful country?" Muhammad asked as he sipped his coffee.

"Survivors who washed up on our shores after a shipwreck."

"I see. What are their destinations?" Muhammad asked.

"Portugal."

Muhammad, realizing it was unwise to ask too many questions and recalling he owed the ambassador a favor, or two, studied him for a moment. He finally said, "I'll have Alayah prepare them for you. Do you want them delivered to the embassy?"

"If you don't mind, I'll wait for them."

"As you wish. What are the names of the refugees?" Muhammad asked as he poised his pen to write down the names.

"John Doe, Joe Blow, and Jane Snow," the ambassador said.

Muhammad raised his brow, "Common spelling I presume." he said.

"Yes, common spelling. How long will the process take?" the ambassador asked hoping to avoid answering any more questions.

"Ten minutes, I'll see to it!" Muhammad stood, "You wait here. I'll get the visas and be right back."

True to his word, Muhammad returned within ten minutes and handed three exit visas to the ambassador. "Here you are, my friend," he said with a smile.

"Thank you. I owe you one."

"Not at all. I think I still owe you," Muhammad replied. Then with a note of conspiracy in his voice, he added, "I've been hearing some unsettling reports that the Nazis are conducting an all-out manhunt for the individuals who destroyed their ammunition depot. The Vaterland's credibility is on the line. No one is immune."

"Capisco!" the ambassador responded with a wink. "You take care, as well."

The two men embraced as the ambassador left Muhammad's office. Alayah was carefully watching their every move. Alayah copied the names he typed on the visas on a slip of paper and tucked the paper into his pants pocket. As soon as the ambassador left, Alayah took a break. He swiftly moved through a narrow alleyway behind police headquarters to a shabby hotel and went to a predesignated room. There he met with a nefarious acquaintance he knew only as *Dagger*.

Alayah's employment put him in a position to acquire information regarding what was happening around Tangier. He was paid handsomely for providing interesting tidbits to the dark side. Money was Alayah's god and he had no conscience regarding the consequences of his actions. This time it involved the identification of the perpetrators of the most egregious event in the history of German warfare.

"What's going on?" Dagger asked in a serious voice.

Alayah relayed what he knew and handed Dagger the slip of paper with the three names on it. After studying the names, Dagger said, "Could these three be the ones the Nazis are looking for?"

Alayah shrugged. "Two men and one woman. You decide for yourself." He rubbed his hands together. *If they are, I may be able to retire.*

• • •

Back at the embassy, Ambassador Edmondson summoned Wagner to his office. As soon as Wagner entered, the ambassador handed him the three exit visas. "There's still time to catch the night train," he said. Concern was evident in his voice.

"We dare not stay too long in one place," Wagner responded. "We're ready to leave."

"Just so you know, Chief Muhammad told me the Nazi military is in town looking for the saboteurs. The sooner we get you out of here, the better—for you and me!"

"Roger that!" Wagner retorted. "I'll round up Becker and Lina."

"The sooner, the better! You'll be pleased to know that after breakfast this morning, Salman arranged for the other refugees to be taken to their respective embassies. They should be safe by now. I'll have him bring the car around and immediately take you three to the train station. Remember, time is of the essence."

Before leaving, the embassy provided appropriate clothing for the trip along with the train tickets for Wagner, Becker, and Lina. the ambassador told them the U.S. owned and operated the plane from Casablanca to the Lajes Base in Portugal and there wasn't a charge for Americans to fly.

• • •

Waiting for Salman to bring the car around to the front entrance, Wagner, Becker, and Lina stood on the portal with the ambassador. As they waited, they exchanged bittersweet farewells.

Embracing the ambassador, Wagner said, "You went above and beyond your duty to protect us. Words cannot express our depth of gratitude." Choking back tears, he whispered, "You take care," and then he stepped aside.

Taking the ambassador's hand, Lina said, "May

God keep you safe. You'll be in my prayers each night." The ambassador kissed her hand before releasing it.

Becker waited for Lina to move aside. He then stepped up and embraced the ambassador in a bear hug. "It's because of brave men like you that the Allies will prevail. I'm not a brave man, but I admire those who are. You're an inspiration. Godspeed my friend."

The ambassador stepped back, and taking Becker by the shoulders, looked him in the eye. "You, my compadre, are a brave man. Courage is defined as doing something you're afraid to do. You've proven your courage time and time again. Don't ever doubt yourself."

Just then Salman drove up. The trio hurried to the waiting car, and giving the ambassador a final wave goodbye, left the embassy.

Before they cleared the embassy driveway, Wagner looked back. His heart skipped a beat when he saw an official-looking military vehicle turn into the embassy driveway.

"Salman," he said.

"Yes, sir. I saw. My instructions were to get you to the train station without delay. The ambassador will be all right."

"I think we should go back—"

"I follow the ambassador's instructions," Salman said. "His exact words were, 'No matter what, get these three to the train station in time to catch the nine o'clock train to Casablanca.'"

"So, he was expecting trouble," Wagner mused.

"Apparently," Salman said.

Still uncomfortable with the situation, Wagner turned back and was silent the rest of the way to the train station.

• • •

Other than Umar, the chef, and Eva, the housekeeper, the ambassador was now alone at the embassy. He suspected, by the way Chief Muhammad was acting, that Muhammad had figured out who the three exit visas were for. Although the ambassador trusted Muhammad, Alayah, that smarmy, shifty-eyed creep, was another story—and Alayah was the one who prepared the exit visas and he now knew the names, albeit fake names, of the travelers. The ambassador shuddered when he realized the gravity of the situation. If Alayah was a spy, the Nazis probably now knew where the saboteurs were and where they were headed.

• • •

The military vehicle that Wagner saw turning into the embassy driveway was occupied by two

Nazi officers. As soon as they stopped at the front entrance, the occupants of the vehicle jumped out, and took the steps two at a time. Approaching the front door, they began to bang on it. Since Salman was out on a mission, Eva rushed to the door and opened it. The Nazis roughly pushed her aside and stomped into the foyer.

Looking around, one of the Nazis placed his hands on his hips and demanded, "Where's the ambassador?"

Eva was so frightened, she couldn't speak. She just pointed to the ambassador's office door. The two Nazi officers hurried across the marble floor and flung the office door open. Ambassador Edmondson had overheard the commotion in the foyer and was expecting the intrusion. Although panic threatened to engulf him, he was determined not to knuckle under. When the Nazis barged in, he looked up and asked in a casual manner, "Yes, can I help you?"

"Where are they?" one of the Nazis shouted.

"Who?"

"The three saboteurs you've been sheltering."

"There's no one here but me and my help."

"Where'd they go?" the Nazi demanded.

The ambassador sat silent. Even though he knew he'd be tortured, he refused to answer.

"I'll ask you one more time, where are they?"

Even dreading what was coming, the ambassador still remained silent. However, instead of applying torture to the ambassador, one of the Nazis went back out into the foyer. He grabbed Eva by the arm and flung her into the office. Still holding her arm, he twisted it behind her back until she screamed. Smiling an evil smile, he asked the ambassador again, "Is your memory improving?"

The ambassador remained silent. When he heard Eva's arm break, he buried his face in his hands. As she fell to the floor, her screams were replaced by mournful whimpers. In a fit of rage, the ambassador jumped up, slamming his chair back against the wall. When he took a step forward, apparently to go to Eva's aid, the Nazi placed a booted foot on Eva's neck. His intent was clear. The ambassador backed off. It took all of his strength to resist, but he knew if he didn't they'd kill her.

Umar was in the kitchen when he heard the ruckus. Grabbing a butcher knife on his way out of the kitchen, he stealthily entered the hallway. He crept up to the open office door, and after assessing the situation, he gripped the knife with both hands. Extending his arms in front of him, he lunged forward, and with one powerful blow, thrust the knife into the back of the closest Nazi. His victim screamed and clawed at his back as he fell to the floor. When the other Nazi turned to see what was happening, the ambassador used the distraction to pull his revolver from his middle desk drawer. With his finger on the trigger, he brought the gun up with one smooth motion, and expertly placed two shots into the Nazi's torso.

• • •

In the aftermath of the encounter, apparently in a state of shock, the ambassador and Umar stood and stared at the two dead Nazis. Blood was forming in pools around the bodies. When Eva began to sob, Umar directed his attention to her. He had been a paramedic in the military before joining the embassy and had some medical training. "Her arm's broken," he said to the ambassador. Umar and the ambassador helped Eva to her feet. Supporting her as she limped along, they took her to the kitchen and gently sat her down on a chair. Umar knelt and carefully examined her arm with his fingertips. He determined the break was midway between the left wrist and elbow.

"I can set your arm," he said as he rose to his feet. "However, we have nothing on hand strong enough to kill the pain. When I straighten your arm and maneuver the bones together, it's going to hurt like hell."

Eva nodded and whimpered, "Just do it quickly."

Umar pulled a small wooden spoon from a drawer. Placing it on a cutting board, he used a cleaver to chop the spoon part from the handle. He then placed the handle between Eva's teeth. "Bite down on this," he said.

Eva bit down on the handle and grasped an arm of the chair with her right hand. Working as fast as he could, Umar manipulated the bones into place. After aligning them, he took the handle from Eva's mouth and positioned it on her arm to stabilize the broken bone. He tightly wrapped the spoon handle and Eva's arm in a kitchen towel. In the meantime, using the kitchen scissors, the ambassador had cut other towels into strips. Umar used the strips to tie the homemade cast into place while the ambassador made a sling by using several other kitchen towels.

Noticing Eva was sweating profusely, Umar dampened a clean dishcloth with cold water and gently wiped her brow. Hoping to keep her from fainting, he said, "The worst is over, Eva. Just hang on." He relaxed when she gave him a weak smile. He went to the pantry where he kept his personal items and removed a small bottle from one of the shelves. Offering Eva three aspirin, he said, "Take these, they'll help ease the pain." The ambassador poured a glass of water and held it to Eva's lips, helping her swallow the aspirin.

The two men helped Eva to her quarters. Although she was still in a great deal of pain, she told them she would be all right. When they were sure they could safely leave her, they went back to the ambassador's office. They had two bodies to dispose of.

• • •

The ambassador and Umar stood over the dead Nazis pondering how to get rid of them before they could be discovered. The embassy could not withstand the close scrutiny that would follow an inspection. Anything and everything invoking scrutiny would need to be disposed of, and very discreetly.

"Their car is in the driveway," Umar said. "We could load them into their car and drive them somewhere far from here and let the authorities try to figure out who killed them."

"I don't know," the ambassador said.

"Do you think an ambassador would be accused of murder?" Umar asked.

Before the ambassador could answer, Salman rushed into the office. The relief was visible on his face when he saw the ambassador, alive and well. Then, apparently noticing the bodies, he said,

"What in the hell…"

The ambassador sat down behind his desk and motioned for Salman and Umar to sit. "Did you get our guests to the train in time?" he asked.

"Yes," Salman replied. Even though he was anxious about the present situation, he knew the ambassador would tell the story in his own time so he sat and waited.

The ambassador took the bottle of bourbon from his lower desk drawer and poured three generous drinks. He handed one to each of the other two men. As they sipped the heady, amber liquor, the ambassador told Salman the story, concluding with, "Now, how do we dispose of the bodies?"

After a period of silence, Salman said, "We could put the bodies into their vehicle and drive it somewhere in one of the more populated areas in the city."

The ambassador nodded to Umar. "Great minds think alike. That's what Umar suggested."

Salman replied, "It's not likely anyone would suspect the American Embassy of being involved in the deaths when the bodies are discovered."

"Yes," Umar chimed in. "There's a great deal of animosity toward the Nazis among the citizens of Tangier. I suspect that finding two dead bodies wouldn't cause too much concern or raise very many red flags." After a pause, he added, "I also think there probably wouldn't be too much of an investigation by the locals because of the Reich's jackbooted tactics."

Setting his empty glass aside, the ambassador said, "It sounds like it could work." Apparently eager to get the deed done, he stood and said, "Come on, let's get to it."

• • •

It was a dark, overcast, moonless night that threatened rain. As soon as the three men loaded the bodies into the military vehicle, Salman said in an authoritative tone, "I'll take the lead and drive their car. Umar, you follow me in the embassy's car. Ambassador, you stay here and keep an eye on Eva."

"But I—" the ambassador began.

Salman cut him off midsentence, "If we're caught, it would be better that you aren't involved," he said as he climbed into the Nazi vehicle. Umar was already in the embassy car and ready to go. "We'll be back within the hour," Salman said, as he pulled his jacket close around him. Before closing the car door, he pointed to the embassy entrance, instructing the ambassador, "You go back inside and lock the doors."

The ambassador nodded and stepped back away from the cars. He watched the two vehicles transverse the driveway. Thankfully, it was late and there was no traffic. He kept vigil until they were out of sight, then he went back into the embassy and locked the door.

Since it was a chilly, rainy evening, the ambassador was grateful that earlier, before leaving for the train station, Salman had made a fire in the fireplace. After checking on Eva, the ambassador went to the pantry and gathered some cleaning supplies. Taking them to his office, he cleaned up the blood. After he finished cleaning, the ambassador tossed the rags into the fireplace. Because of the chemicals he used to clean the marble floor, the rags instantly burst into flames and completely burned, leaving no trace, only ashes. After returning the cleaning supplies to the pantry, he went back to his office to wait.

• • •

Upon leaving the embassy, Salman drove to one of the main thoroughfares. If this was going to look like a retaliatory killing, he wanted the victims to be in plain sight and appear to have been accessible to the phony killers. Salman pulled to the curb and carefully looked around. No one was in sight. Probably, the late hour and threat of rain had kept the night people inside. The street was virtually empty. Umar stopped the embassy car behind the one Salman had driven. He ran to the military vehicle and helped Salman put one of the bodies into a position behind the steering wheel. The other body was already in the passenger seat.

Taking their time, they examined the interior of the military vehicle to ensure nothing was left to incriminate the ambassador. Once they were satisfied it was clean, they drove back to the embassy. When the ambassador heard them drive up, he rushed to meet them at the door.

Before the ambassador could speak, Salman said, "Mission accomplished. That's all you need to know." After a pause, he asked, "How's our patient?"

"I checked on her about an hour ago. She's sleeping," the ambassador replied. "Thank you."

"I wasn't much help—"

"Not just for Eva," the ambassador said, emotion apparent in his voice.

"It's my pleasure to be of service to you. However, from this point forward, don't mention this incident again. If we're interrogated, we didn't see or hear anything," Salman said. For a fleeting moment, Salman reminded him of Solomon.

• • •

The coconspirators spent several anxious days waiting to see if anything disastrous was going to come from the Nazi deaths. The third day after having discovered the bodies, Chief Muhammad paid Ambassador Edmondson a visit.

When Salman ushered Muhammad into the ambassador's office, the ambassador said, "Come in, come in and take a seat." Although the ambassador knew full well what the visit was about, he asked, "To what do I owe this pleasure?"

Muhammad removed his service cap, and placed it under his left arm, as he sat down. "I was in the vicinity and decided to stop and say hello." Obviously, watching for a reaction from the ambassador, he continued, "I suppose you heard about the murders that happened three days ago."

Instantly on full alert, the ambassador sat up straighter, his mind was filled with dread. *Does he know?* "If you mean the Nazis, yes, I heard about that. Do you have a suspect yet"

"Well, yes and no," the usual implacable Muhammad said.

"Yes, and no? Hmm, very intriguing. Am I privileged enough for you to share details?"

"Of course," Muhammad said as he sat back. Casually crossing his legs, he placed his service cap on his bent knee. "It appeared Alayah was somehow involved," he blurted.

"Alayah?" *That creep! How appropriate. No*

telling how many deaths he was responsible for.

"Yes, Alayah. It appeared he was working both sides of the street. After preparing your exit visas, my sources informed me that he sold the names you used on the visas to both the Nazis and the black market. Since the war, the Tangier black market has been making a killing selling forged exit visas. Apparently, not wanting to lose their source of income, after Alayah was exposed, in order to protect their operation, Alayah had to be eliminated." After a pause, Muhammad added, "They got to him before we could make the arrest."

"That's unfortunate. However, I can see why Alayah was killed, but I don't understand the reason the two Nazis were also killed."

"The assassination has all the earmarks of the age-old territorial struggle. It's assumed that the Nazis decided they wanted to send a message to the black market to stay off their turf. However, they underestimated their nemesis. It appears that the black market was alerted. The Reich is not the only ones who have spies. Their scheme backfired, literally, and the two officers were caught in the crossfire. I believe it was the Nazis who got the message." He looked sternly at the ambassador.

"After my men discovered the Nazi bodies, we examined them and discovered one was actually stabbed, not shot. Not wanting to confuse the Nazis any more than necessary, we put a couple of bullet holes in that one's chest. The way the blood from the stab wound had spread, unless one looked closely, the blood could have been from gun shots."

The ambassador then realized Muhammad knew about the Americans and that he was covering for them. "Thank you," the ambassador said. Then catching his *faux pas*, he quickly added, "For coming by that is."

"No thanks necessary. However, there is one interesting question no one can answer."

"Oh, what's that?" the ambassador asked, trying to keep his voice calm and maintain his composure.

"The ambush had to have occurred after dark. I was informed by the Nazi criminal investigator that the officer occupying the driver's seat, couldn't drive after dark. His night vision was impaired." From the look on the ambassador's face, it was obvious Muhammad knew he had struck a nerve. The implication wasn't wasted. The ambassador was skilled at reading between the lines. He knew exactly what Muhammad was inferring.

Muhammad stood and put his service cap on. Glancing toward the door, he said, "Well, I must get back to headquarters. We're pretty busy right now."

The ambassador walked Muhammad to the door. Muhammad paused before going out, "Being the police chief has its advantages. Since you're the one keeping score, I believe you now owe me one—a big one," he said and stepped out into the foyer, closing the door behind him.

The ambassador stared at the closed door for a moment. *Amen to that, my friend, amen to that!*

Chapter Fourteen

Destination

The train ride from Tangier to Casablanca took approximately two hours. Wagner, Becker, and Lina hoped their luck would hold out long enough to get them to the airfield in Casablanca and then to the U.S. base in Portugal.

Since the embassy had provided them with train tickets, they bypassed the line, and easing their way through the crowded station house, went directly to the platform and boarded the train. Still exercising caution, they refrained from sitting together on the train. Their plan was to regroup at the station house when they arrived in Casablanca.

Wagner was now in the habit of looking at everyone with skepticism. The word trust was no longer in his vocabulary. The enemy came in all shapes, sizes, and colors. They were now too close to home to take unnecessary chances. Like the legendary Wild Bill Hickok, Wagner chose to keep his back to the wall. He took the last seat in the train car where he could see the other occupants. Lina was several seats in front of him but still in his line of vision.

Swarms of people kept pouring in and when the train appeared to be filled, the conductors began closing the doors. Feeling safe, at least for now, Wagner leaned his head against the bulkhead. He was thinking of home and a reunion with old acquaintances. Lost in his memories, he was startled when suddenly the train whistle emitted a shrill blast. Wagner jerked upright and peered out the window. The train was moving slowly from the station. The platform was crowded with what Wagner presumed to be family and friends waving and shouting as the train chugged past. Picking up speed, they soon cleared the station and left Tangier behind. It was now too dark to see the countryside they were traveling through so Wagner turned his attention to the other passengers. He struggled to determine who was friend and who was foe. His efforts were not working so he gave up trying. For now, until proven otherwise, they were all foe.

• • •

There were several Nazi military personnel aboard. Seated together, they good naturedly laughed and chatted among themselves. Wagner wasn't close enough to hear their conversation, but a couple of them kept looking toward Lina. When one of the Nazis stood and approached her, Lina turned her head away. Ignoring him, she concentrated on looking out of the window. The Nazi was not that easily put off. He bent and whispered something to the woman seated across from Lina. The woman immediately rose and left the car. The Nazi took her seat.

Leaning forward with his elbows on his knees, the Nazi said to Lina, "Hey, Beautiful, where are you going?"

Lina gathered her jacket close around her, pretending not to hear. Wagner, gripping the arms of his seat, was on full alert as he watched and waited.

Tapping Lina's knee with his knuckle, the Nazi repeated his question. "Where are you going?"

Realizing there was no escaping the encounter, Lina said, "Home."

"Home? And just where is home?" the Nazi asked and looked back at his buddies, obviously to ensure they were also paying close attention to his pickup tactics.

"Lisbon," Lina said, hoping to end the conversation.

"Ah! Lisbon, one of my favorite cities," said the Nazi. "What is your favorite place in Lisbon?"

Lina had never been to Portugal, much less Lisbon, and didn't have a clue as to what was there. However, she did know that Jesus's mother,

Mary had a shrine dedicated to her near the city of Lisbon. "Our Lady of Fatima Shrine," she said and made the sign of a cross. "I'm a nun returning home."

"A nun!" the Nazi exclaimed. "Why aren't you wearing a habit?"

Lina pretended to cry. "It was awful! My clothes became torn and soiled when I fled a war zone. The church in Tangier gave me these," she said and looked down at her garments.

"I see," the Nazi said. "Please forgive my intrusion." He then stood and went back to his seat where his buddies were waiting.

Still watching, Wagner relaxed a bit when he saw the encounter had ended. *Wonder what she told him?*

• • •

When the dejected Nazi approached his comrades, one asked, "What happened?" Disappointment evident in his voice.

"She's a nun. I'll not disrespect the sanctity of a nun!" the Nazi said and sat down.

"Since when?" asked one of his detractors.

"Why, you…" the first Nazi snarled. He stood, and without warning, punched his offender in the face. Blood squirted from the offender's nose.

Putting his hands to his face, the offender

howled in pain. The first Nazi, with raised fists, was standing in the aisle, ready to finish the fight. However, their comrades intervened and separated them. One of their comrades admonished the two fighters, "Don't we have enough enemies to fight? Why do we need to fight each other. Now, break it up or I'll have you both court martialed."

"You're right," said the aggressor. "I'm sorry," he apologized and offered his handkerchief to his injured comrade.

Accepting the handkerchief, bloody noise replied, "Me, too. I was way out of line."

The fight ended in a kumbaya moment and the participants shook hands.

Nonetheless, Wagner remained on high alert. Since the three refugees didn't have identification, if the military police were to get involved, no telling where it would all end. *God willing, in a little over two hours, we'll be in Casablanca.*

Wagner's prayer was answered. They arrived in Casablanca on time and without any further incidents.

• • •

Casablanca, like Tangier, was neutral, which meant those supporting the Axis as well as the Allies were welcome. Wagner suspected the Nazis were still looking for the tunnel saboteurs so the three of them would need to be constantly vigilant and take no unnecessary risks.

Because of the war, Casablanca had become the melting pot of the world. Wagner, Becker, and Lina regrouped in the station house, where they blended in with the other travelers. It appeared that people of every nationality had converged on Casablanca. The place was a jumble of people wearing colorful native dress and speaking various languages. As they stood in the midst of the confusion, their challenge now was how to find the airport without raising suspicion.

"Any ideas on who we can trust to get directions?" Wagner asked.

While they pondered their situation, Lina noticed the Nazi she encountered on the train standing a few feet away. "I have an idea," she said. Before Wagner and Becker could stop her, she briskly turned and approached the Nazi. Wagner and Becker, having been taken by surprise when Lina walked away, anxiously watched the exchange.

Approaching the Nazi, Lina said, "Pardon me. Perhaps you can help me."

Immediately recognizing Lina from the train, the Nazi pulled his cap from his head. Clutching it to his chest, he responded, "How may I be of service?"

"I must catch the plane to Lisbon. How do I get to the airport from here?" Lina asked.

"Do you have an exit visa?" the Nazi asked.

"Ah, yes. The church provided one for me."

"Excellent." Stretching his neck, looking over the top of the crowd in the station house, he said and pointed, "There's a bus that goes directly to the airport. It leaves here shortly after every train arrives. It stops in front of the door, right out there."

Lina looked the direction the Nazi was pointing. "Oh, thank you—"

"You're welcome," the Nazi said. He then pulled a wad of French francs from his pants pocket and pressed them into her hand..

Surprised, Lina said, "Oh, thank you, but I can't accept—"

Putting his forefinger to his lips, he silenced her. "God bless you, Sister. Pray for me." He whispered and then turned and walked away.

Lina, stunned that the encounter went so well, stood for a moment. When she turned and saw Wagner and Becker looking in her direction, she immediately rejoined them.

"Come with me," she said. Then opening her fist, showing them the French francs, she said, "I even have money to pay for the bus." Surprised, Wagner and Becker just stared at her. "Come on!"

she said, sounding somewhat annoyed at their reluctance, and led them to the bus stop.

• • •

The airport wasn't as crowded at the train station. In fact, there were scant few people waiting for the plane. It appeared leaving by plane wasn't as easy as by train. When the trio approached the ticket counter the attendant looked up and frowned.

"Your destination?" he asked in a curt manner.

When Wagner started to say something, Becker, fearing an altercation, intervened. "Portugal," he said. "The U.S. base at Lajes Field."

"Exit visas," the attendant said.

Becker looked at Wagner with that *Don't you dare!* expression on his face. Wagner nodded and handed the attendant the three exit visas. The attendant studied them for a moment, and much to Wagner's surprise, stamped them and handed them back. No questions asked.

"The plane is boarding," the attendant said and pointed to an open door. "Do you have luggage?"

"No," Wagner replied.

"You're cleared to board," the attendant announced. Then he added, "Godspeed."

Does he know who we are? Wagner thought as they walked to the plane. Confiding in his cohorts, Wagner said, "That was much too easy. What'd you think?"

"Don't look a gift horse in the mouth," Becker replied. "We deserve a break!"

With their track record, Wagner surmised, they'd probably be shot down over the Mediterranean. However, the plane trip from Casablanca to Portugal was completed without incident. When they landed at the U.S. base at Lajes Field, they were met by the base commander.

"I was informed I'd be escorting some Americans back to the States." the commander said. "I'm Commander Logan and I'm very happy to meet you."

Wagner, still in a state of euphoria at actually having made it this far alive, couldn't speak. Becker made the introductions. Lina was introduced as an integral part of the team. As they walked to a Jeep, Commander Logan said, "My instructions were to get you back to the States ASAP. Unfortunately, it's not safe to fly outside of American airspace, but we do have a battleship leaving tomorrow bound for the States. She's due for an overhaul.

Apparently dreading another adventure at sea, Becker asked, "How long will the trip take?"

"Depends on the weather and how many German U-boats we have to dodge," Commander Logan replied.

I knew it was too good to be true, Wagner thought.

Noticing the expression on Wagner's face, the commander laughed. "Relax, Partner. You're pretty safe here. Ol' Betsy will get you home."

The strength and courage of old reasserted itself and Wagner's confidence returned. Anxiety was history. There was a promising tomorrow. A new era was in the offing!

Chapter Fifteen

Conclusion

The trio spent the night aboard the battleship and it was underway before dawn the next day. Lina had her own quarters, the men shared quarters with the ship's crew. Traveling on a 50,000-ton battleship was far different than bobbing around the sea in a lifeboat. The refugees actually enjoyed the experience. They shared their time on the lifeboat, without revealing too much, with the ship's crew. At mealtime they were the life of the party, so to speak, and everyone seemed to enjoy their company.

Because Lina was with Wagner and Becker, no one questioned her nationality. Even though she spoke with an accent, it was assumed she was American. One evening, as the trio stood at the rail watching the waves, Lina said, "When we arrive, will I be allowed to just walk into your country?" She desperately wanted to become an American citizen.

"Probably not. There is a process that immigrants must go through. I'm not sure what all it entails," Becker responded.

"Oh…," Lina said. However, she didn't complete her thought. Her disappointment was evident. "I think I'll try to get some sleep," she murmured as she headed for her quarters.

After she left, Wagner and Becker were alone on deck. Becker turned to Wagner and said, "I heard that, under the War Brides Act, spouses are allowed to enter the U.S. without going through the immigration process."

"Okay," Wagner said and knitted his brow. "How does that help our situation?"

"You sure are thick-headed," Becker responded. Turning, he leaned his back against the railing and looked at Wagner. "I know you love her, why not marry her before we get to the States. The ship's captain can perform the ceremony."

"Whoa! Hold on, Buddy. You're right! I do love her, like a sister. Besides, I'm not the marrying kind," Wagner said. After a pause, he added, "However, I'll be your best man."

"What?" Becker croaked.

"Knock it off! I've known you too long. You can't fool me. You're the one who's in love with her."

"Is it that obvious?" Becker asked.

"Yep, to those who know you, it's that obvious." Wagner punched Becker on the biceps. "If you agree, I'll go ask her to join you up here. It's a beautiful moonlit night…"

"Okay, okay. You win." After a pause, Becker asked, "Don't happen to have a three-carat diamond on you, do you?"

"Sorry, Pal, fresh out," Wagner replied and turned to leave.

Before he was out of earshot, Becker shouted, "This has been quite a ride. Thanks. Thanks for everything."

Wagner turned and saluted Becker. "You're welcome. However, I should be the one thanking you."

• • •

Lina hadn't gone to bed yet when Wagner rapped on her door. "Yes, who is it?" she asked.

"It's Wagner. Becker wants to see you. He's still up on deck," Wagner responded.

"What? Are we in trouble again?" Lina asked, her voice laced with fear.

"Oh, no. Nothing like that. Just go see what he wants," Wagner said and turned toward his quarters.

Lina frowned. *Those two must have gotten into the grog.*

When Lina approached Becker, he turned to face her and took both of her hands in his. "Close your eyes," he said.

"Close my eyes?"

"Yes, close your eyes and pretend we're on a million-dollar yacht floating around the Caribbean. We just popped the cork on a bottle of wine. A warm breeze is blowing and in the distance, we can see silhouettes of the palm trees against the moonlit sky. The air smells of sweet perfume, soft music is playing in the background, and the heaven is filled with a billion stars."

Stepping back, Lina frowned and asked, "Are you alright?"

"I'm more than alright, I'm terrific. Just keep your eyes closed and indulge me," Becker said and continued his scenario, "You're looking beautiful in an expensive designer gown and I'm very handsome in my black tux. Now, I take you in my arms, like this," Becker said and pulled her close. Lina didn't resist. "I whisper in your ear, Lina, I'm in love with you. Will you marry me?"

"Are we still pretending?" Lina asked in a husky voice.

"No, this is for real. Will you marry me?"

Throwing her arms around Becker's neck, Lina asked, "You're not just doing this to get me into the U.S. are you?"

"No! That would be a cheap trick and I wouldn't do that. I meant every word I said. I want to spend the rest of my life with you. Will you do me the honor of being my wife?"

"Yes! Yes, yes, yes," Lina blurted.

When Becker pulled her closer, she whispered, "Be careful, you're wrinkling my expensive designer gown." She then kissed him tenderly.

Wagner had been lurking in the shadows. When Lina accepted, he punched the air with a closed fist. *Good job, Becker. You were right, I do love her but you'll make a better husband.*

About The Authors

Judith Blevins' whole professional life has been centered in and around the courts and the criminal justice system. Her experience in having been a court clerk and having served under five consecutive district attorneys in Grand Junction, Colorado, has provided the fodder for her novels. She has had a daily dose of mystery, intrigue and courtroom drama over the years, and her novels share all with her readers. In addition to the ten novels in **The Childhood Legends Series**®, she has authored or co-authored thirty-four adult novels.

Carroll Multz, a trial lawyer for over forty years, a former two-term district attorney, assistant attorney general, United States Commissioner, and judge, has been involved in cases ranging from municipal courts to and including the United States Supreme Court. His high-profile cases have been reported in the **New York Times**, **Redbook Magazine** and various police magazines. He was one of the attorneys in the **Columbine Copycat Case** that occurred in Fort Collins, Colorado, in 2001 that was featured by Barbara Walters on **ABC's 20/20**. He recently retired as an Adjunct Professor at Colorado Mesa University in Grand Junction, Colorado, where he taught law-related courses at both the graduate and undergraduate levels for twenty-eight years. In addition to the ten novels in **The Childhood Legends Series**®, he has authored or co-authored thirty-six adult novels and eight books of nonfiction including his recently released handbook entitled **Testifying in Court—A Guide for Peace Officers**.